The Robots of Cottage H

The Robots of Cottage H

E. E. "Doc" Murdock

H.O.T. Press
Publishing fine books since 1983

H.O.T. Press
Los Angeles, California
www.hotpresspublishing.com

ISBN: 0-923178-35-X
ISBN-13: 978-0-923178-35-2

Books by E.E. "Doc" Murdock

Novels

- **God's Messenger – God's Victim**: A *Bildungsroman* Stockholm Syndrome Novel
- **The Pain Artist:** An American Hikikomori
- **My Vietnam War**
- **A Psalm for Cock Robin**: A Harp and His (Dead) Mother Mystery
- **Crueltown**: A Drew Steele Los Angeles-Las Vegas Mystery
- **The End of the Civil War**: A Drew Steele Civil War Mystery
- **Who Owns Arizona**: A Drew Steele Civil War Mystery

Textbooks/How-To Books

- **How to Write Fiction: Tools and Techniques**
- **Self Management: A Guide to More Effective Study**
- **Computers Today**
- **Computers the Easy Way**
- **Windows the Easy Way**
- **DOS the Easy Way**
- **HyperCard the Easy Way**
- **dBASE the Easy Way**

History/Political Books

- **From Washington and Adams to Hillary and Trump:** The Stories behind the Story of Every Presidential Election, With Special Focus on the *Volatile* Presidential Election of 2016

- **Obama Won, but Romney Almost Was President:** How the Democrats Targeted Electoral College Votes to Win the 2012 Presidential Election

Acknowledgments

I am indebted to the members of the Ojai Writing Workshop who provided valuable feedback as I worked through the many drafts of this book. I would also like to acknowledge the help of all my students at California State University, Long Beach who taught me so much. And of course, in the end, it was Zoe that made this book happen.

For Zoe,
without whom this book would not exist,
and without whom I would not exist.

The robots are taking over. People must be warned.
(From my soon to be published smash hit bestselling book, ***The Robots are Taking Over***)

Chapter One

"Sounds. I'm hearing sounds."

"We've been through this before, Mr. Scott. I understand how real a dream can seem, but If I'm to help you, we need to focus on reality. Now, we were talking about your childhood. May we continue that?"

A dream? Not real? No, can't be. Feels like reality to me. Sounds are real, aren't they? I'm hearing sounds, rhythmic sounds. Like . . . tires on pavement? Am I in a car? Force eyes to open. Look outside head.

Yes, I'm in a car. A fast-moving car. Real trees going by. Real plowed fields. A real sun just coming up.

And there is pain. Pain is real too. Pain in face. What happened? Did someone hit my face? And pain in both wrists too. Feels cold, like metal. Brain says cold metal on wrists must be handcuffs. Wrists handcuffed behind. Means I must have got arrested again. What did I do this time?

Use eyes. What are you seeing?

Two cops in front seat. One has light skin, the other dark skin. They seem human, but the robots have gotten so good at creating skin-like coverings you can hardly tell anymore. Until I'm sure, I should just do what I always do, play along, pretend this is really happening.

But wait, maybe I need to take some kind of action. I should try to find out where these two cops are taking me. If they *are* robots, I could be in big trouble. Maybe they found out I'm going to write a book about how they plan to take over the world, so they're taking me somewhere to dispose of me.

Dispose. That's how robots would think about getting rid of a troublesome human.

But wait. How did I come to be in this police car?

Use brain. Remember.

A bar. I was in a bar. But how did I end up in that bar?

Think.

Go back further.

I woke up. Dark. Must have been nighttime.

What woke me up? An idea. Inspiration? Yes, that's it—an inspiration woke me up. It was an inspiration that I should write my book about the robots like it's a story. Get more people to read it that way. Get them to know the truth before it's too late.

Wait! I actually started writing that book, didn't I? What happened to that writing?

Think.

Remember.

After I had the inspiration, what did I do?

I crawled out of that alley. Managed to stand up. Dizzy. How long since I ate anything? No way to know. I leaned with both hands against the brick wall. Had to get going. People need to be warned.

People on the street stared at me, then quickly looked away. Did they think I was dirty? Well, how would they look after yet another night of sleeping in a dirty alley? And so what? Only ordinary dirt. No big deal. Easily rinsed off in any gas station bathroom, even though that means walking around all day in wet pants until they dry. No big deal. Done it before.

But what would father say?

He doesn't care. If he cared, he wouldn't have thrown me out.

Ran fingers through greasy hair like a comb. How did hair get so long? No comb. Didn't I once have a comb? A blue comb. What happened to that comb? Years ago. Long gone.

Never mind that. Not important. Think. Remember.

"I was walking. Searching."

"Are you having a memory about searching, Mr. Scott? Is it a childhood memory? Tell me more about it."

Why is she always doing that? I'm right in the middle of trying to remember something when all of a sudden, she pops in. I'd better straighten her out. "No, not a childhood memory. It was night. I was walking. The streets were deserted."

"Nighttime? And where were you going?"

"Paper."

"Paper?"

"Yes, I was looking for writing paper. I had an inspiration. Write my robot book like a story."

"So, this memory is about a book? And it's a book you say you're going to write?"

Going to write? What is she implying? That I won't ever get it written? I am writing it. I'm writing it right now. This is it.

Aw, who cares if she believes me? I should just ignore her.

It was night. I was walking. Looking for paper. The streets were deserted. That's odd. The streets of this city are never deserted. Why aren't there any people in this reality?

Don't think about that. Just keep remembering. Walking, trying to keep my new story-telling method clear in my brain until I could find some paper to write it down. Unsteady. Probably a bit too much to drink yesterday.

Yesterday? No memory of a yesterday. But there must have been a yesterday. There's always a yesterday, isn't there?

Stumbled into the first bar I came to. Dark in there. Such places all look the same: long narrow room, worn wooden floor, men lined up at the bar on stools, hunched over, staring into their drinks. And there's always a TV blaring behind the bar, going on and on about the president and how he's ruining the county. Politics. Same old crap. Who cares about that?

Those bars all smell the same too: old spilled beer, sweat, uncontained urine.

Spotted a small table in the back. Even darker back there, but probably enough light to write by. And lots of little square napkins in a holder on the table. Napkins are made of paper. Robot story can be written on those little pieces of paper.

Went to that table. Sat down. Searched pockets. Damn, my stub of a pencil is gone. Did the robots take it? No, probably not. Robots don't have any need for a pencil.

Bartender came over. Hoped he wasn't a robot. Asked him if I could borrow a pen. Please.

He asked if I was going to buy a drink. Said it like he didn't believe I had any money. Had I been in that bar before? Did he know me?

Tried to act normal. Said, Kind sir, what is the cheapest thing you have to drink?

Water.

Undeterred, I asked again. Beer? At least?

Draft beer is cheapest.

How much?

Three bucks.

I turned away from him. Dug into pants pockets.

Nothing.

Try shirt pocket.

Aha! Some change.

Count it.

Ninety cents.

That's it? That's all the day's panhandling netted? Out there in the cold all day long, paper cup in shaking hand, please on my face, pretty please, just a little spare change?

Gave that bartender the ninety cents. Said, Can't I just get a small glass of beer?

He went away.

Came back with a *really small* glass of beer.

But he also brought a pen.

I laid the napkins out in a neat row. Started writing the new story-like version of my book about how the robots took over:

A young genius named Scott gets a job at Oracle Computer Company. In the Innovations Division. He's a computer programmer, and he got a big signing bonus, along with an apartment in the company's downtown high-rise building.

At work, Scott has his own cubicle. With a window. He looks out his window at the teeming city far below, and he's happy. He's proud to have moved so high up in the world right out of Harvard College.

He looks at his computer watch that notifies him about how much money is being deposited, minute-by-minute, into his personal bank account. It means he's arrived in the big time. After being a starving student for so long, he can now buy just about anything he wants. But what should he buy? He can't think of anything, so he just asks his Intel-Based Oracle Advanced Advantage Pure Lightening Computer that question.

It responds with, "Given your salary and your important new position in the world, you should get one of the amazing new My Man Friday Mr. Everything household robots from Google's Advanced Intelligence Products Division. At a special price for this week only! Save money by acting now. Just think how much easier your life will be with your very own Mr. Wonderful personal servant!

Free money-back guarantee if you're not completely satisfied.

Scott thought, Well, why not? Everybody is talking about these fancy new household robots. I should celebrate my new position by getting one.

As if the computer had read his mind, it said, Sure, why not? Go for it. If you don't like it, you can easily return it for all your money back, and because it can walk away on its own, there is no return shipping charge.

Scott decided the computer was right. Household robots were damn expensive, but so what? He can afford it now. And wouldn't it be something to have your very own robot servant? Everybody is saying these new household robots are supposed to be even better than a human servant. He tells the computer to go ahead and order it, and have it delivered to his new apartment.

That's as far as I got. A big guy got off of his stool at the bar. Came over to ask what I was writing.

Told him I was writing an important book. No time to talk. The robots are taking over. People must be warned.

Big guy said he would buy me a real drink if I'd tell him what I was writing.

I suddenly felt very thirsty. One drink couldn't hurt.

Bunch of drinks later, I'd told him quite a bit about the book. Told him it's true story. How the robots are taking over.

He laughed. At least it proved he wasn't a robot. (Robots don't laugh.)

You're crazy, bud. (Called me bud. That's okay. Better not let anybody know my real name.)

But I'm not. Crazy, that is. There really are robots all around us, even if nobody else knows it but me. I told the big guy he was dumb for not seeing it.

That's when the big guy started hitting me. Not fair. Big guy like him, hitting on skinny little me. But then bullies have always picked on me. Ever since I was little. It's because they realize I'm smarter than they are.

I did what I always do: don't fight back. No matter what you might have heard, it doesn't work to hit back at big bullies. Just makes 'em mad, so they hit you even harder. Best thing is to laugh. Say, Ha, ha, you can't hurt me. Not what they want to hear. Sooner or later they'll give up and stop hitting you.

But for some reason, this big guy didn't stop. Kept on hitting me.

So I guess that's why my face hurts.

At some point, he knocked me down, so I curled up on the floor to try to protect my vital parts. He started kicking me. So I guess that's why my ribs hurt.

Cops showed up.

Big guy ran away.

Cops wanted to see my ID.

Don't have ID.

Why not?

Because I don't want the robots to be able to track me.

What robots?

Didn't answer. In case *they* were robots.

What's your name, bud?

He called me bud too, same as the big guy. Okay with me. Better to not let them know my real name. I said, I've decided not to have a name anymore. Who remembers names anyhow?

What's your address?

Harvard College.

Harvard College? Are you sure? Let's see your Harvard College student ID.

Don't have it.

Why not?

Taking a break from my studies. For a while.

How long of a break?

A few years. Maybe a bit more.

That means you're homeless.

Homeless is a category, I said. I refuse to be a category just because I don't have a place to live.

Okay, I remember it all. Now it all makes sense. Those cops put these handcuffs on me and put me in the back seat of their police car, the police car I'm in right now.

If this cop car really is the real reality, I'd better take action. Try to get myself out of here.

I'll use my magic powers to transport myself to somewhere else, somewhere where these robot cops can't find me.

Where should I go? Sure could use another drink. I'll transport myself back to that bar.

I concentrate on my teleportation routine.

Hmm. Doesn't seem to be working correctly. Put me somewhere else. Where am I? Looks like I'm in some kind of fancy office with lots of books on shelves, and I seem to be lying on a couch.

"Are you ready to continue, Mr. Scott? It says in your chart that you were a student at Harvard. A student athlete. It also says that at times you can be quite articulate, but sometimes you tend to go silent. Can you tell me why you do that?"

Now I get it, I'm back in that shrink's office. Why did my magic transporting beam bring me back here? And why do I have the illusion that she's talking to me? I know she's not real.

Oh, now I get it. Robot Central Command must have intercepted my particles during the transformation process and sent me here. The question is, why didn't they want me in that police car? Maybe the robots weren't controlling those cops after all. I should have stayed in the back seat of that police car. Only logical. I'd better transport back there.

There, that's better. I'm back in the police car. And we're still on the same highway. And a too-bright sun is just peeking over those distant hills. Means it's a brand new day. I like it better when there's daylight. Not so dangerous. Not so many scary things lurking around.

But where are these cops taking me? Better find out.

I sit forward to talk to them through the metal mesh screen type thing that separates my back seat world from their front seat world. I say, Listen, your honors, I didn't start the fight in that bar. Honest. And even if I did, it's only because I'm a writer, so bar fights are necessary. Raw material, you see.

Did they even hear me? It's like I didn't even talk.

Well, maybe I'd better not talk to them anyhow. You never know, even though they look like regular human cops, they could be robots. Better to not let them know I'm on to them.

"I'd better not let them know this is the real reality."

"I'm glad you realize that, Mr. Scott. Yes, this is real. You are safe in my office. You seem to have a tendency to doubt the reality of your situation, a tendency to feel you are in danger. There's no need for that now, Mr. Scott. You are quite safe. Now, let's get back to what we were talking about. You were telling me about your childhood. Can we continue with that?"

What the hell is she talking about? My childhood? I remember my childhood very well. In fact, I remember it all. I remember it all the way back to even before I was born, when I was still inside my mother. But I'm not going to tell her about that. Why does this shrink think childhood is so important anyway? The main thing is not to her confuse me.

What was I thinking about? Oh, yeah, the real reality. This cop car.

I'd better try to figure out where these cops are taking me. Maybe I shouldn't have even tried to talk to them. I should just sit back and keep quiet. Maybe they're only taking me to the jail-house drunk tank, as usual.

"The drunk tank's not such a big deal."

"The drunk tank? Are you referring to a special section of a jail for inebriated prisoners, Mr. Scott? Would you say you have a drinking problem?"

Now what's she up to? I'm always having to straighten her out. "It's not exactly a problem. I've been there plenty of times. The drunk tank, that is. It always starts with me having too much to drink, and sometimes that leads to me getting arrested. Benders. That what some people like to call them. I don't mind the somewhat inaccurate term, as long as they add the qualifiers, going on a. Nothing wrong with going on a bender once in a while. Whenever I can panhandle enough money to pay for it. Just letting off a little steam. Like in that old cartoon that showed steam coming out of a guy's ears."

Hey, maybe I'll find a way to use that image in my book about the robots. As soon as I get the wherewithal.

Wherewithal. That's a good word. I should write that word down. Sure wish I had my hands free of these handcuffs so I could be writing down all these good ideas I'm having.

But I'd better not get distracted with that right now. Somebody said I have a tendency to get distracted. I need to keep focused on the here and now.

But what is the here and now?

Think. Focus on what's real.

Oh, now I remember. I got arrested, and the cops put me in the back seat their police car. That's the reality, not that weird woman shrink. Whoever heard of a woman shrink anyhow? Always trying to get me to live in the past. I don't want to live in the past. I should just go along with the this police car ride. Nothing wrong with going on a nice car ride in the country. And what happened last night in that bar doesn't matter either. It's in the past too. Past is gone. Might as well be forgotten. Present is what counts. Better look around here in this present. Figure out what this version of reality looks like.

Well, it looks exactly like what it is: I'm still stuck in a cop car, handcuffed and sitting on a hard plastic bench-type seat. Hey, why would robot cops make their back seat out of hard plastic? Guess robots don't understand the concept of human comfort.

But wait. Something's wrong with this reality. Whenever I have a little too much to drink, the cops take me to the downtown police station. But we're going *out* of the city. Where are they taking me? To a drunk tank in another city?

Now they're slowing down. Turning off the highway. A few houses nearby, but still no big city in sight anymore. They're driving up a curving driveway that has nice green grass lawns on both sides.

Better sit up. Get a better look.

The driveway leads up to what looks like a bunch of red-brick buildings scattered across a flat area on top of the hill. Most of the brick buildings are not all that big, but the one in front is pretty big. It has a fancy tall column with white stone filigree (is that the right word?) attached to the top of it. Gets me to wondering: did that column used to be an old bell tower? No bell in it now. Maybe it was a church at one time. Now it looks more like an old-fashioned castle. Did they ever make castles out of red bricks?

Hey, why are the cops bringing me to this place instead of taking me to the downtown jail? Is this some kind of out-in-the-country jail?

But wait, now I see a sign stuck in the lawn: East Aurora State Hospital.

State Hospital? Aren't state hospitals where they send crazy people? Don't think I want to be here. I don't belong in a mental hospital. I'd much rather go to the police station, even though I'd have to spend yet another night trying not get beat up while lying shivering on the very cold, very hard concrete floor that slants down from all directions to the stinking piss and shit and vomit hole in the middle.

If these two cops are taking me to a mental hospital, it must be because Robot Central Command told them to. It means the robots do know I'm onto them. Maybe this is where they take the humans that have figured out what they're up to. Clever way to get rid of humans without having to kill them. Maybe robots don't like to kill us humans because we invented them. Maybe they're programmed to not kill humans. It's a hopeful thought.

Actually, this East Aurora State Hospital place doesn't look too unfriendly. Green grass. A few regular-looking people walking between the buildings. Not so bad, at least not when it's being seen from the too-hard back seat of a police car which you're very ready to get out of because you've thrown up on your own lap, not once, not twice, but three times, the last being the kind of throwing up where there's nothing left but acid bile that burns your throat.

That reminds me: when did I last eat? Saturday? Sunday? What day is this anyhow? Do days still exist? (I've always suspected somebody else was making up time, not me.)

The car stops. The cops drag me out, being kind of rough, and they're making mean jokes about me being a smelly son of a bitch. Why are they mad at me? It was my lap that got thrown up on, not theirs.

Now they're complaining that they'll have to hose out the back seat when they get back to the station.

Now I get it: the back seat of their car is made of hard plastic so they can hose it out. Logical. Exactly how robot cops would think.

As they drag me toward the building, I look around. Seems like it's going to be a nice day.

But wait, shouldn't it be a dark and foreboding day? Maybe raining or something. Or does it being a nice sunny day mean this situation is going to turn out all right? Is it up to me? I know I create reality, so why am I creating this particular version of it?

Too many questions. Got to stop thinking random thoughts. The robots are taking over, and I need to warn everybody. Need to write my book, focus only on what is real.

But are my thoughts actually random? Maybe the robots figured out how to control my thoughts.

No, that can't be. I'd know if they were controlling me, wouldn't I?

The cops pull me up the too-bright white concrete steps and then through the wide front doors of the castle-like brick building. They pull me to a scarred wooden counter where a sourpuss old woman robot with fake reddish-brown hair is staring at me from behind a clear plastic barrier. She has a permanent frown on her face. Are they making robots with that kind of face now?

The sourpuss woman puts a piece of paper into a metal tray, and then the tray rotates until the paper comes out from under the clear plastic barrier.

The light-skinned cop takes the piece of paper out of the tray, gets a pen out of his pocket, and starts to fill out it out. It's some kind of form.

He turns to me and says, Hey, bud, why don't you carry any kind of ID? They searched me earlier. Found that my pockets were empty except for a broken rubber band, a lot of pocket lint, and a few pieces of napkin with some indecipherable scribbling about robots. Hey, maybe those notes were how Robot Central Command found out I was onto them. Well, if they're already onto me, I might as well answer his question. I say, I don't carry any ID because I don't want Robot Central Command to know who I am.

Robots? he asks, why are you always going on about robots?

Don't play dumb with me, mister cop. You know the robots want to assign us all a number so they can match us all up with their cameras and their fancy face-recognition software. They've got photo-surveillance in places we humans would never expect it. Like in bathrooms because robots don't care about such things as privacy.

The cop stares at me like he's pretending he doesn't know what I'm talking about.

Yeah, go ahead and act dumb, mister cop. But you know what I'm talking about. They're always watching us. Spying on us. Like when I was using a computer at the library. Robot Central Command figured out it was me online. They tried to trick me into logging on using my real name. Said I had to make up a password. Had to be at least eight characters. At least one capital letter and one special character. Rules. That's how I knew the robots were behind it. Everywhere you look these days it's rules, rules, rules ever since the robots started taking over. Rules about where we humans can go and where we can't. Rules about which side of the road you *have to* drive on, which I would ignore if I had a car that hadn't already been destroyed a long time ago by breaking exactly those kind of rules. So you see, your robot tricks won't work on me. I'm onto you.

Both of the cops are staring at me now, acting like I said something strange. Maybe I shouldn't have said all that. If they are robots, or if they're working for the robots, maybe they can get around the rule of not killing a humans if the human is judged to be dangerous to them. Maybe they could get permission to per-manently decommission me.

Better act more undefective.

I smile at the robot cop and shrug to show him I'm not really all that crazy.

The cop shakes his head, frowning. He must still think there's something's wrong with me.

"But actually, I'm pretty darn normal."

"You say you feel you are normal, Mr. Scott? Tell me more about that."

Should I explain it to her? Well, why not?

"Well, I'm pretty darn normal compared to most people any-how. I might not be considered totally normal if you're basing normalcy on being one of those show-offs that've climbed up to the pinnacle of the classic normally-distributed, bell-shaped curve of normalcy, but I'm also not flung out to the edge of that curve either."

"You know about bell-shaped curves?"

"Sure. I studied about that kind of stuff during the year I was at Harvard College. I was there for a whole year before the robots got me kicked me out for—you guessed it—not following their rules. But even though their robot rules kept me from completing my college education in their big-shot Harvard College Psychology Department, I continued my own education by reading all of the psychology books they have in the big downtown public library where I spent most of my days last winter. When winter came, I had to stay there in that library to stay warm. And I had to keep on reading in order to stay awake. Fall asleep even for a moment and the meany robot woman in charge of that library would come and throw me out. She said I had to sit up straight and keep on reading or else she'd send me back out onto the cold streets. So I stayed there all day, way back in the darkest part of that library. Reading psychology books. It was warm in there, and besides, I was learning a lot of good psychology stuff I could use later. After the library closed at night, I always headed for my secret place in the bushes under the freeway, that place where the highway crosses over a dry riverbed. But then winter came, and it started to get too damn cold out there at night. I was freezing my ass off, so I went looking for a better place. Found an alley downtown where there was a back door of an open-all-night Chinese restaurant. A little bit of wet heat came out of the screened vent that was cut into the bottom part of their door. Lots of Chinese food smells came out too. A little warmer there by that door, but let me tell you, those food smells just about drove me crazy with hunger. They wouldn't give me any of their precious Chinese food until late at night when they finally came out to toss the leftover food from people's plates into the dumpster. I'm pretty sure they knew I was climbing into that dumpster and eating their tossed-out food, but they didn't try to stop me."

"Well, that was quite a story. Mr. Scott. It sounds like you've been through some hard times. Do you feel that it may have contributed to your, shall we say, your current condition?"

Condition? What condition? What the hell is she talking about? Life hasn't been all that bad for me. I'm still alive and kickin', aren't I? She's trying to distract me again. I can't let myself get distracted. I need to make sure I keep thinking about what's real and what isn't.

Uh oh, I'd better pay attention to the cops because I think the light-skinned cop is trying to get me to tell him my name, and I think he's already asked more than once.

I'd better try to act more non-defective.

Scotty Scotch, I say, loud and clear.

The cop says, Really?

"Yes, Scotty Scotch is my real name."

"Is that the name you want to go by, Mr. Scott? Does it make you feel like a different person?"

Damn, now I'm back in that shrink's office again. I've got to get better control over my teleportation system.

"Mr. Scott?"

"Uh, it's so the robots can't trace my movements."

"Robots again. You feel you have to use that name because of the robots?"

"Sure. It's a good fake name. It'll confuse them. They'll associate it with the drink of the same name humans like to consume, and they'll think maybe I'm not actually defective, only that I've consumed too much of the human Scotch-type drink. I made up that cool fake name when I was still a kid. Back then, I liked to pretend to be somebody else. I'd hide under the bushes in the park and make my secret plans. Usually, I was a secret agent hiding from my country's enemies. I stayed there hiding in the dark until everybody else was asleep. Then I could go out and sneak behind enemy lines when they least suspected it."

"A childhood memory of when you pretended to be someone else. Can you tell me more about that?"

"Well, okay. Like this one night, I was doing what I did, being a superhero. I was hiding in the bushes, waiting for my chance to strike, when Mom and Dad found me there. They pulled me out of the bushes, and boy were they mad at me. I guess it was because I hadn't come home for supper. They went on and on about how I was always spoiling things with my weird behavior, and how this time I'd spoiled things for my little brother who was all set to go see a Disney cartoon movie that evening. Sorry, I don't remember the name of the movie—maybe something about a princess and a prince that liked her."

The cop is asking me a question: Scotty Scotch? Is that really your name?

I shrug. Who cares whether he believes me or not. He may not even be real. And if he is, he's probably being controlled by the robots.

He writes it down on the form. Then he asks for my address.

I give him the fake address I always give, the address of the house with the magic window.

It was a wonderful house. In the same neighborhood as the real house I grew up in.

"I always wished I lived in that house because of its magic window."

"A house? With a magic window?"

Her again. Why is this woman shrink always wanting to know about my childhood? I'd better tell her something. "Yeah. I discovered that house early one morning when I took a different route to school. I was oh, maybe about ten or so. That day, I stopped to look at a very tall house that had a tiny little window up close to the top of its peaked roof. I knew immediately it was a magic window. If I was able to be up there and look out that window, I knew I could control anybody walking by down below. If I could have lived in that house, I would have spent a lot of time just looking out at the world through that little window, knowing I could control all of the little people down there if I wanted to. To this very day, I always try to think of the world that way, as if I'm looking down on all the little people, seeing them from way up on high, controlling them."

"You feel you can control people? Using magic?"

"Sure, If I want to. But I don't always want to. Sometimes, I just let them do whatever they want to. So I can watch them and learn about human behavior."

The shrink writes something in her notebook. What is she always writing in the notebook. Is she going to turn it over to Robot Central Command? I'd better be more careful what I say.

I'd better pay attention to what the cops are doing. The cop has finished writing down my fake address on the form, and he's written down a bunch of other stuff too. I wonder what he wrote. I hope he didn't write something about me acting crazy. That could get me in trouble. Big trouble.

The cop puts the form back in the metal tray, and the sour-puss robot woman behind the clear plastic barrier rotates it back in to her side.

Nothing left for me to do but stand still and wait, for what I don't know. All I know is that it's a different world now. Anything can happen now. I wonder what the alien beings who watch us from up there on other planets think of the robots taking over down here on this planet. Maybe they'll come down and save us. But maybe not. Maybe they don't care about what us puny humans are up to. Hard to predict alien beings. They come and go. Always turning on their invisible cloaks so nobody can see them.

Uh oh, better not get lost in those kinds of thoughts. Better keep your eyes and ears working on the here and now.

I look around. What kind of place is this state hospital?

Gloomy, I'd say. Ugly green dirty-looking walls. With my special powers of observation, I can tell it's been a long time since the walls were painted. No paint smell. Smell is a good way to tell what's real and what's not. If I can smell something, it means it's real. Probably. And there are no pictures on the walls.

"At the police station, there are pictures of dead cops all along the wall."

"Are you having another memory, Mr. Scott?"

Geez, is she always listening? I'd better say something. Don't want her thinking I'm a crazy person. "Yeah, I was remembering the cop station where they took me when I had a little too much to drink. There was a hallway where you have to wait until they book you into the drunk tank. They handcuff you to a railing that's so high off the floor you can't sit down or even squat, so all you can do is stand there and look at pictures of dead cops. Killed in the line of duty, the sign said."

"Is this a recent memory? Have you been arrested often?"

Careful. Don't answer that. Man, if she only knew how many times I've been arrested. Actually, I've been arrested so many times I've lost count. In fact, by now they know me at that police station. They all call me the robot man.

The important thing now is to check out this new place they've taken me to. At that police station, there are no windows, but here in this mental hospital place there is a window. It has bars on the outside of it. Are they afraid somebody trying to get in, or is it to keep me from getting out? Should I be worried? Should I be trying to find a way to escape?

"But wait, now I notice another window."

"You are remembering a window? Is it that magic window you saw high up in that house?"

Should I tell her about it? Oh, why not?

"No, this is a new window. High up at the end of the hallway, right up next to the used-to-be-white ceiling tiles. The window is kind of dirty, but I'm pretty sure it's a stained-glass window."

"A stained-glass window? Are you imaging you are in a church?"

"It is like the ones they have in churches. You know, made out of colored glass pieces that have all been pieced together to create a picture. Makes me wonder if this mental hospital really did used to be some kind of church. But in the few churches I've been inside of, on food-hand-out days, their stained-glass windows are usually pictures of praying angels with hazy halos around their heads, or else maybe a big tall God with a long white beard, his arms spread wide as if welcoming everyone to heaven. It's a little hard to make out exactly what the picture in this stained-glass window is because it's so dirty and it's so far up there by the ceiling, but I think it's showing a giant red-colored Devil with a long black pointed tail."

"So, you are saying you once saw a stained-glass window that seemed to be showing a red-colored Devil?"

"Yeah. The Devil is standing high up on what seems to be a cliff. He's got his hands on his hips, and he's staring down at a bunch of naked screaming people that are all tangled up together. Like a ball of writhing earthworms. He's laughing at all those people because they're being perpetually burned in hell's fires with no chance of escaping it by dying."

"Quite a dramatic picture, Mr. Scott. Did you actually see such a window somewhere?"

"Yes. It's kind of hazy, but it's real."

"Are you sure you actually saw such a window, Mr. Scott?"

What is she trying to do, convince me that I'm imagining things? I'm seeing the stained-glass window of that Devil with my very own eyes, aren't I?

Jesus, what kind of thing is that to have inside the entrance hall of a mental hospital? Why couldn't they have the kind of stained glass windows they have in those churches, pictures of kindness and peacefulness? But no, the robots in charge of this place have created a stained-glass window of a Devil. I think they must be trying to scare the shit out of us humans. But why?

"What are they trying to say? Abandon all hope ye who enter here?"

"That's a famous line from literature, isn't it, Mr. Scott?"

Oops, did I say that out loud? I guess she doesn't know where the line came from? I'd better fill her in so she doesn't think I'm making things up. "It's a line from Dante's *Divine Comedy*, one of the books a professor talked about when I was in a literature class during that year I was at Harvard College."

"Would you say that book has influenced you, Mr. Scott?"

This shrink has no idea of what I'm going through. But then, she's probably not even real. I'd better test that. "I know you can't keep me here for very long. I bet you'll do what they always do when the police send me to a shrink, always, by the way, a male shrink. Now that I think about it, a male shrink would make more sense. Maybe I'm making up a female shrink."

"You feel you are making me up?"

Darn, did I say that out loud too? I'd better change the subject. "Listen, what you don't seem to get is that my alcoholism is not a symptom, but only a cause."

"I see. Tell me something, Mr. Scott, do you ever hear voices?"

Here she goes again. "Uh, what kind of voices?"

"Perhaps voices that aren't really there."

"That doesn't make sense. If the voice is not really there, then how can I hear it?"

"Well, sometimes people imagine they are being spied upon. For example, do you think the CIA is spying on you?"

"Of course they are. Isn't that their job?"

"All right. Good point. But what about fantasies? You said you believe you can control other people. Do you ever have fantasies of killing people?"

"Who doesn't? I wouldn't be normal if I didn't think about that sometimes. Like the politicians on the TV. Everybody wants to kill them. They go on and on and on and—"

"All right, Mr. Scott. I get your point. But let me ask you another question. Do you ever think about hurting yourself?"

"No. Why would I want to do that? It would hurt."

Why am I answering her dumb questions anyhow? I'm beginning to suspect that maybe she's also a robot. Have they started taking over the shrinks too? Would robots want to be shrinks? They probably wouldn't even understand why us humans would want to have mental illnesses.

Anyhow, I'm sure my answers to the shrink's questions have proved to her that I'm not crazy. But earlier she said they were going to have to hold me for thirty days. For observation, she said. After they observe me for a while, they'll get tired of asking me questions. Same as at the cop station.

Actually, I wouldn't mind hanging around this mental hospital place for a few days. At the police station they had pretty good food, at least compared to what I'm used to. If they decide to keep me here in this place for a while, I might even get a real bed. But sooner or later, they'll have to let me go, and I'll be back on the streets again.

"The streets. Not an easy place to survive."

"The streets? Are you referring to the unfortunate situation of being homeless, Mr. Scott?"

Hmm. More questions. Better straighten her out. "The streets are not easy. But I have my tricks. And my magic powers. I'm pretty experienced with street life because I haven't had a home to go to since my dad threw me out. He said if I was going to act so crazy as to get kicked out of college after he paid all that money, it was time for me to go out and find my own way in the big bad world."

"So, you got kicked out of your home. Did you resent your father for doing that?"

"Well, I've been out in that big bad world he was referring to for quite a few years now, and maybe I haven't done all that great, but I'm still alive and kickin' aren't I? He said I was too crazy to know when to come in out of the rain. Well, he was wrong, dead wrong! If it rains, I have my secret places to go to stay dry. Like that library. Warm and dry in there. And lots of books to read. I like books. I like the feel of them in my hands, and they're full of amazing stuff."

"Yes, books are good. I was told you are somewhat well read. But we were talking about your father. Did you have a lot of books in your home when you were growing up?"

"Some. But they were silly."

"Silly books?"

"Yeah, kid books."

"I like grown-up books, especially the psych books I read at that library. I learned lots of stuff about humans in those psych books, stuff that the robots wouldn't understand."

That stopped her. Does she think I know more about psychology than she does? I probably do. If I was the shrink and she was the patient, I wouldn't be asking her such dumb questions. Better not let her get me distracted with her dumb questions.

Uh oh, now I see a door open at the far end of the hallway. Two big men in not-very-clean white uniforms come through it, and they're coming straight toward me. This can't be good. The guy in the lead is a pretty big black guy, and he looks kind of mean. Right behind him is an even bigger white guy who looks even meaner. Are they coming for me?

As they get closer, I can smell them. Sweat. Thank goodness. It means they're real humans. Robots don't sweat. In fact, robots don't smell like anything, except sometimes you can pick up the very slight odor of overheated electronics coming from inside of them.

The cops take the two big guys aside, and they talk in whispers. The light-skinned cop gestures toward me with his thumb, and says something about robots. Is he telling these two big guys about the book I'm going to write? That might not be good. Maybe I should just leave. The front door is standing wide open, and I'm even skinnier than when I used to be a real fast college runner. I bet I could run right out the front door of this place, and they'd never catch me. I guess it might be a serious handicap to run with my aching wrists handcuffed behind me, but maybe I could still do it.

"Used to be I could run all day and not get tired."

"Ah, so now you're ready to talk to me again? Yes, I read in your chart that you were a runner. A college athlete, in fact."

Why does she always want to know about my past? Maybe the robots are using her to find out more about me so they can figure out how to control me?

I'd better be careful with what I say to her.

"Yeah, I went to a really big high school which was good because I could pretty much be anonymous there and not get beaten up so often. But I guess I wasn't quite anonymous enough because one day when I was out watching some soccer players, a big bully started picking on me, and had to run away from him. A coach saw me running and took me aside. He said I looked like a pretty fast runner, and he wanted me to try out for the school's cross-country running team. I told him no, I'd rather just stay anonymous. But he said it was an order. He said I had to stay after school that day because he was going to hold cross-country tryouts on the track that went around the football field. He said all the fast runners in the school would be there. I didn't want to get into trouble, so I did what he said. But I didn't do so well in his first tryout because I figured if I ran faster than any of the other guys, they'd wait until the tryouts were over and beat me up. The coach pulled me off the track and asked me why I was running so slow when he'd seen me running fast on the play-ground. I told him the only reason he'd seen me running fast on the playground was because I was running away from a bully that wanted to hurt me. The coach said if I didn't get back on that track and run faster than the other boys, *he'd* tell them to beat me up. So I got back on the track and ran faster than all the other boys. Anyhow, that's how I ended up on the cross country team. I won a lot of races to keep from getting tripped and knocked down by the runners from the other schools, and that's how I got into Harvard College. They recruited me to be on their cross-country running team. Even gave me a partial scholarship."

"But you didn't stay at that college very long, did you? Can you tell me why that was?"

"Well, a lot of the other students at that college, and even some of the teachers, thought I was a smart-Alec. But honest, I wasn't trying to be a smart-Alec, I was only trying to straighten them out. Ever since I was a little kid, I've always thought that when I could see that somebody was on the wrong track, I should straighten them out. I'm only trying to be helpful, but it's a habit that keeps on getting me into trouble. Like that big guy last night in that bar."

"A bar. I'm sorry, Mr. Scott, but you couldn't have been in a bar last night. You were here in this hospital."

What? She's getting confused again. Better ignore her. I know where I was last night, and she doesn't. In fact, I don't know why I keep talking to her. Her and her fancy suit and her fancy office and her fancy leather couch. Fancy pictures of her with other people up there on her tall bookshelf. In one picture, she has another person standing next to her. They are both dressed in white, and both are holding tennis racquets. I knew kids at that college like her. Kids that thought they were big shots because they knew how to wear white clothes and play tennis.

But who cares about her? I don't even know why I'm imagining her in such detail. She's not important because she's not part of the real reality. Better keep my focus on what's real.

The guys in white uniforms keep on glancing at me while they talk to the robot cops. Maybe I really should run right out the front door. But why should I? I won't be here long anyhow. It'd be better to get a few free meals and maybe a bed, and then as soon as I convince the shrink I'm not crazy, they'll have to let me go.

Their whispering is over. The two big guys dirty white uniforms come and take ahold of both of my arms. They turn me around so the light-skinned robot cop can remove my handcuffs. After that's done, I'd like to rub my wrists to get some feeling back in them, but no, the two big guys keep a tight hold on my arms. Did Robot Central Command intercept my thought about running out the front door so they directed these two humans to keep a tight hold on me?

The two big guys hustle me off down the long hallway toward the same door they came from. Why are these two real humans doing the bidding of the robots? I'd like to ask them that, and maybe straighten them out, but I don't get a chance to because now we're at the door, and the big black guy is choosing a key from the ring of keys that's attached to his belt by a long stretchy wire. He uses that key to unlock the door, and then they pull me through it.

I'm surprised to see that we're outside again, and there's a too-bright sun creeping higher into the sky. They lead me along a sidewalk that has a lot of cracks in it. There are even a few weeds growing in some of the cracks. As soon as I meet whoever is in charge of this place, I should straighten them out by telling them that a cracked sidewalk with weeds growing in it is not good aesthetic practice, especially as it's likely to be one of the first things us newcomers see after just arriving at their fine mental hospital.

The cracked sidewalk triggers something from inside my brain, a memory.

"A memory. I'm having another memory."

"Another memory? Good. Let's talk about that, Mr. Scott. Is it a childhood memory?"

Now I'm sure she's somehow gotten inside my brain. She seems to be able to hear my thoughts. I'll just stick to telling her my stories, and not let her into my thoughts.

"It might be a childhood story. Something about a crumbling sidewalk."

"A crumbling sidewalk. Very symbolic. Was there a sidewalk in that realistic dream you say you keep on having, the dream about getting arrested and taken somewhere by the police?"

Dream? Watch out. Can't let her get inside my dreams.

"Dream? What dream? No, the crumbling sidewalk was a long time ago. It was in front of an old shut-down factory where I used to wander around all by myself when I was a kid. I always got a kind of scared feeling in that old place, and that was good because fear was as close as I could get to feeling anything real back then. To this day, I remember that feeling well. Gloomy and lonely, like maybe like everything in the world had got destroyed, and this was all that was left. There was a lot of old equipment inside that factory. Abandoned stuff. Idle and rusting away. Reminded me of what old people look like, what they must feel like. Made me think maybe I too would get old someday. But being a kid, I quickly pushed that thought away. I knew I wouldn't ever get old. Now that I'm a little older, I'm even more sure I won't ever get old because . . . well, maybe just because I don't like the idea. I've seen old people, and they don't look very happy."

"You think old people don't look happy? Do you feel you are normally a happy person, Mr. Scott?"

"Well, I am happy, at least most of the time."

Maybe I shouldn't have told her that. Maybe it's not sane to be happy in this screwed up world.

The two big guys in dirty white uniforms are not happy with me. They growl at me and ask me why the hell I keep stopping to stare down at the sidewalk.

I tell them, I'm having an important memory right now that was triggered by the weeds in your sidewalk. You shouldn't have weeds growing up in your sidewalk. Bound to trigger memories in the kind of people the robots are locking up in this place. And why are you helping the robots anyhow?

"Don't you realize they're going to take over?"

"Who is going to take over, Mr. Scott? Are you talking about the robots again? Do you still believe robots are watching you?"

"Of course they are. They pretend to be the CIA, but they're not really. The CIA was taken over by the robots. Like all the rest of them."

"The rest of them? Do you mean the government?"

"Yeah, all of them."

"Do you really believe the government has been taken over by robots?"

"Of course. It makes sense that the robots would start there. Only logical. They started with the president, and then took over the rest."

"I see. You believe the president of the United States was taken over by a robot."

"Sure. It's obvious. Would a human talk like that? And look at that hair. Would any human really have hair like that?"

Now she's looking at me in that odd way again. I don't even know why I bother to talk to her. I've go to stop letting her sneak into my thoughts and keep my focus on what's real.

The two big guys look at each other and shake their heads. Did I say something out loud to them?

They pull me along faster, jerking on my arms and acting real mean, telling me to hurry it up cause they don't have all day.

They don't have all day? What else do they have to do? Isn't this their job? I'm about to straighten them out about that, but before I can do it, we arrive at another brick building. The guy with the keys unlocks the big wooden door, and they escort me into a fairly narrow corridor with grime-streaked walls that are painted the same ugly dark green color as that first place. And still no pictures of dead cops on the walls. Nothing at all in the corridor except for several big heavy-looking chairs with gray-colored padded plastic seats and shiny chrome arms. The chairs are lined up against the wall. Only one guy is in the chairs, and the two big guys sit me down hard right next to him. The big guy sitting next to me doesn't even look at me. He's just staring straight ahead. I figure he must be an incoming patient like me, also waiting to see the shrink. He's dressed in gray sweat pants and a white sweatshirt that has dark-stains on it (blood?). His sweatshirt has black printing on the front of that says, At Least I'm Not You, which I don't take personal because he doesn't even know me.

The two big guys go off, and at the far end of the corridor they disappear around a corner. Must be another room down there. I get up to go see, but before I can get there, the black guy looks back around the corner and points at me. He says, Sit!

Okay, fine with me. I'll sit. I guess they want me to sit here until they can get me in to see the shrink.

As soon as I'm seated again, I do a little fingers-wiggling wave at the staring-straight-ahead guy and say, Hi, I'm Scotty.

He slowly turns his head to look at me. But then, he turns his head back, just as slow, to resume staring at the ugly green wall. He's working his mouth, like he's chewing on something. Maybe the inside of his cheek. Reminds me again that I'm hungry. Can't remember when I last had something to eat.

A little guy comes around the corner. My acute powers of observation tell me he's barefoot. I also notice that he's dressed in baggy black pants and a dirty-looking white undershirt that has holes in it.

Odd. Why don't they dress their patients better in this place? Assuming he is a patient.

He heads right toward me, but in a kind of sideways shuffle, like he's not sure he wants to get too close to me. But he is grinning, and that probably means he's not a robot. As far as I know, Robot Central Command hasn't made any robots that grin. His grinning makes me think he must have just heard a great joke. I wonder if he's coming to tell me the joke.

When the little guy gets closer, he stops and just stands there in front of me. He's an odd sort. A little bird kind of guy. Probably timid, but with intense laughing eyes. Must be patient. Real crazy, I bet.

He points at me and says, Dangerous?

He said it like it was a question. Is he asking if I'm dangerous? I decide to play along. I say, You bet. I'm the Durango Kid. A killer. Kill ya soon as look at ya.

That seems to relax him. He sits down next to me, still grinning. He says, That means you're not. He points as his feet. They call me Barefoot Billy. Ask me why I don't have any shoes on.

Okay, Billy. Why don't you have any shoes on?

They took them away from me.

Why did they do that, Billy?

They think I'm dangerous.

Are you?

Naw.

Does that mean you are?

Yep. But not as dangerous as that guy. He points at the guy sitting next to me and whispers, He's thinking about going right out through that door. Billy points at the big wooden door.

I shake my head and say. That door is locked, Billy. I saw them lock it after they brought me in.

No, I mean he's gonna go right *through* that door.

You mean he's going to try to break out?

Barefoot Billy sits back and says, Yep.

I look at the door and say, Seems pretty solid to me.

It is, says Billy, but that guy doesn't want to be in here. He feels trapped.

You've talked to him?

Tried to, but he won't talk.

So what makes you think he's going to—

The big guy jumps up and runs straight at the door, and I'm kind of stunned when that big wooden door hardly even slows him down. The part of the door around the lock shatters, leaving the lock hanging and the door ajar.

Amazing! Barefoot Billy was right, the guy ran right through the door.

I jump up to see where he went, and I make it out through the door in time to see him run past the next-door brick building. Then he's off down the grassy hill, moving fast. He seems to be a pretty good runner, and I'm curious to see if anybody is going to stop him.

But no sooner do I walk around the edge of the building to see where he went, when I hear a voice yell, Got ya! And I find myself flat on my face on the sidewalk. I hope my nose isn't broken.

When they pick up off the sidewalk, I see it's two guys wearing guard-type uniforms that have ahold of me. They have their own police in this place? Are they robots?

Hey, I say to them, Why did you tackle *me* instead of chasing after the big guy that broke your door and ran away.

They don't seem to want to answer my question. As they lead me back toward the building we came out of, I look them over. One of them, the one who has an iron grip on my arm, is a lot bigger than me, but the other one is short and very thin. His cop-type shirt is so big on him that his hands are almost hidden inside the too-long sleeves. He doesn't look like a robot, but who knows, maybe they're making all kinds of different-looking robots now.

When the two guards get me back to the building, the little guard points at the shattered wood of the door and says, How'd you do that? He seems pissed off at me.

I smile my best smile at him, the one that almost always works and say, I didn't do it. It was the other guy. He ran right thought the door. You shoulda seen it. Amazing. I just went out to see if he made it all the way down the hill. He did. Got clean away.

The little guard glowers at me. What're you talking about? What big guy?

I nod toward the row of empty chairs in the hallway and say, He was sitting right there when they brought me in.

Barefoot Billy is still there, leaning up against the ugly green wall, hands in his pockets with an I-told-you-so smug look on his face.

I say, Tell them, Billy. It wasn't me that broke their door. Tell them it was that other guy.

Billy just grins (what *is* the joke he's thinking of?).

The two guards drag me down the corridor and around the corner into a large room that has a lot of those same heavy-looking chairs. Almost every chair has a guy sitting in it. None of them look very happy. Are they all new incoming patients like me, other guys who got captured by the robots?

The guards lead me past all those guys, right up to a old beat up gray metal desk where a sullen-looking older man with too-pale skin and too-black hair is sitting looking through some papers. He's wearing a tired-looking black suit, so I figure he must be the one in charge here.

Maybe I can explain to him that it wasn't me that broke his door.

The little guard puts both of his hands on the desk and says, This guy tried to escape. Broke our door.

Tired-black-suit-guy looks up at me.

No, I tell him, real quick. It wasn't me. It was the other guy. He ran right through the door.

The little guard guy spins his finger around next to the side of his head.

No, wait, I say, I'm not nuts. That other guy broke your door. He got away. Ran down the hill.

Tired-black-suit-guy sorts through his stack of papers which makes me wonder if he's looking for my form, the one the cops filled out when they brought me in to that entrance place.

He seems to find the form he's looking for and looks at it for a few seconds. He says, Cottage H without even looking up at me. Then, he goes back to sorting through his papers.

I hear a laugh from behind me and turn to see it's Barefoot Billy. He's grinning at me.

"Okay, Billy. What's the joke?"

"Was Billy one of your childhood friends, Mr. Scott? Was he important to you?"

Here we go again. She's always asking more and more questions about my childhood, and always writing down more stuff in her damn notebook. What if she's compiling a complete history of me to turn over Robot Central Command? There's no other explanation for all her weird questions. But maybe I should humor her. Make up something to throw her and the robots off the track.

"Uh, well, let me think. Billy. Billy. He must have been that kid who fell through the ice."

"A childhood friend of yours fell through some kind of ice? Tell me about that."

"Well, it was winter, and there was this river that froze over. I used to go out there to stand by it and listen to the water going by under the ice. I liked to think about what it was like under that ice with the river still flowing by down there but not going anywhere up on top where I was. One day, another kid came along. It was really cold, but he was only wearing a sweatshirt, not a heavy coat like me. His sweatshirt had words on it that said he should Just Do It, but I didn't know what those words meant. What was it telling him he was supposed to do? Anyhow, he didn't seem at all cold, even though I was. He said, 'Watch this,' and he ran and slid way out onto the ice. Then he came back and said, 'Now you try it.' I was a little scared that the ice might break, but he'd done it, so I figured I should try it too. Anyhow, I ran and then slid out onto the ice, but not as far as he did. He laughed and called me a chicken. He said, 'Watch this,' and he ran even faster and slid way out onto the ice. Then the ice broke and he fell through. He was just . . . gone. I yelled to ask if he was all right, and he yelled back that he was. He said it wasn't so bad under the ice. He said there were other kids down to play with, other kids that had fallen through the ice over the years. After that, I sometimes went back out to that river to talk to him. He was always there, and he always said I shouldn't worry about him because he was having a lot of fun down there under the ice playing with all the other ice kids."

"Now is that really a true story, Mr. Scott. It doesn't get cold enough around here for a river to freeze over. Exactly where did this take place?"

"Oh, well, it wasn't around here. It was way up where it's real cold. In . . . uh, Alaska, I think. I went up there once when I was a kid. Just to look around."

"Mr. Scott, please. If you are going to tell me your childhood stories, I would appreciate it if you could stuck to actual facts."

So, she doesn't believe me. Well, so what? It's a totally true story. Or at least as true as any childhood story. What do we actually remember about our childhoods anyhow? I bet she doesn't remember anything about her childhood. If she even had a childhood.

Maybe she's actually some new type of female shrink type robot, and as we all know, robots are not born and don't have childhoods. They're built in a factory.

Besides, why should I care if she believes me or not? Lying on this couch in this shrink's office is all probably just some kind of weird dream anyhow.

I again want to ask Barefoot Billy what the joke is, but the two guards don't give me a chance to. They walk me back down the hallway and past a workman who's trying to fix the broken door.

Back out into the bright sunshine, the guards lead me to a smallish brick building that's isolated way over at the far edge of the grounds. It doesn't seem like the kind of place where the hospital shrink would have his office. The building's front door has a big letter H painted on it, and the door is made of gray steel, not wood like all the other doors I've seen in this place. Is there something different about this building?

The little guard raps on the door, and after a short wait, the door is opened by yet another big guy (why do they have so many big guys in this place?). I'm pretty sure this guy is not a shrink because, firstly, he's not wearing a suit and tie like all shrinks do—he's wearing a white shirt and black pants—and secondly, he's got a wooden baseball bat in his hand. To hit people with? That must mean he's not a robot. Robots are so strong they don't need baseball bats.

Baseball-bat man pulls me inside without a word to the guards. He slams the door closed in their face, and then he gets ahold of my elbow and leads me down a short hallway to another door. He unlocks that door and swings it open. It's not a very big room, and its cluttered with cardboard boxes. Seems to be some kind of storage room.

He pushes me inside and uses his baseball bat to push me toward the back of the room where there's a big pile of clothes. The clothes are clearly not new, and for some reason, the idea sneaks into my head that these are the clothes of former patients.

Why did the patients leave behind so many clothes? Did they die?

Baseball-bat man says, Okay, let's get those clothes off you.

So he *can* talk. His voice is like gravel, the voice of a tough Army drill sergeant. Now that I think about it, he even looks the part—pock-marked square face, close-cut dark hair, squinting eyes. Not that I've ever been in the military, but he seems like the tough sergeant type I've seen in old war movies.

He again uses his bat to push me forward, and I say, Hey, quit pushing me with that bat. It hurts.

He laughs a short mean laugh and says, It hurts? Really? He again pushes me forward with the bat, even harder this time.

I tell him, Yes, it does hurt. Who the hell are you anyhow? What right do you have to push me around with a damn baseball bat?

He laughs again. Who am I? Why I'm your houseparent. This is Cottage H, and I am the houseparent of Cottage H. It means I'm the one in charge here. Get it?

What the hell is he talking about? Houseparent? Is this how it works in this place? They lock patients in these brick buildings they call cottages with a mean person who calls himself a house-parent.

He pokes me again with his baseball bat.

I hold up both of my hands. Okay, I get it. You're the house-parent of Cottage H. So am supposed to act like you're *my* parent?

This time he doesn't laugh, but he does put a snide-looking grin on his face. He says, That's exactly right, new guy. My name is Mr. Trump.

Trump? Is his name really Trump? The same as the person they're always talking about on TV?

He says, But you can call me Dad.

I say, Dad?

He says, That's right. From now on, you are to call me Dad.

So this baseball bat guy who claims his name is Trump wants me to call him Dad.

Weird. No way I'm going to do that. I say, Sorry Mister Trump, but I've already got a dad. He may not like me very much anymore, but he's still my dad.

He swings his bat at me.

It hits me on the side of my arm, and I yell, Hey, that hurts! I rub my arm to try to make some of the hurt go away. I think I'm going to have a bruise.

Now the baseball bat guy is again doing his grin that's not really a grin as he says, Yeah, it hurts. That's the idea. Consider it your first spanking from your new dad. And you'll get a lot more spankings from me until you learn the rules. We like order around here. Peace and quiet. Get it?

My arm still hurts, but I grin right back at him to show him I can grin too without really meaning it. I say, Well, Mr. Dad Trump. I should tell you right now that there's been some kind of mistake. If this Cottage H is like a mental ward, then I shouldn't be here. A ward is for crazy people, and I'm not crazy. I haven't even been to see the shrink yet. The shrink will tell you I'm not crazy. He'll tell you I don't belong here. He'll tell you there's been some kind of mistake made.

Now Trump is not laughing, or even doing his fake grin. A mistake, eh? Well, I'll tell you what the mistake is. The mistake is yours, for not following my orders. Like I said, here in Cottage H, we like things nice and orderly, and I'm the one that gives the orders. Now take off your clothes. He shakes the baseball bat at me.

Obviously this Trump guy doesn't get it. They can't arrest me and take me right to a mental ward without me getting to explain to a shrink that I'm not crazy, not really. But I'm starting to think this Trump guy might actually hurt me bad with that baseball bat of his, so I decide to go along with him. For the time being. No use getting hurt in my first five minutes in this so-called cottage. And after all, my clothes *are* pretty stinky. I kick off my shoes and pull off my shirt and my throwed-up-on pants. I drop them to the floor.

The Trump guy again threatens me with his baseball bat. He says, Take everything off. Right now! Even your underwear.

Gladly, I say, and do as he says.

He kicks my stinky, vomit-smelling clothes into the corner and stands back, looking me over. Is he deciding what size clothes to get me?

Suddenly, he laughs out loud, at what I don't know. Is he making fun of me? My male protuberance might be, shall we say, a bit on the smallish side, but it's not very nice of him to make fun of it. I decide to ignore his impoliteness and just stand there, all naked, while he digs through the pile of clothes.

He pulls out a black hooded sweatshirt and tosses it to me. It has the faded words Just Do It on the front. I think I've seen those words somewhere before, but I still have no idea what they mean. Just do what? And why did he pick that particular sweatshirt for me? Is he implying I should do something? Oh well, I decide wearing an old sweatshirt with weird words on it is better than standing around naked. As I put it on, I realize it smells a little musty, but I have to admit it is better than the throwed-up-on smell of the clothes I just took off.

He uses his foot to push a pair of tight-fitting, yellowed underpants toward me. I'd almost rather go without underwear than put on those underpants that obviously used to belong to someone else, but he's the one with the baseball bat, so I again decide to keep my mouth shut. I put them on.

He looks me over, and then he begins to dig deeper into the pile of clothes. Finally, he pulls out a pair of worn-looking black sweat pants and tosses them to me. I can see that they're way too big for me. Is he that bad at judging sizes, or is he intentionally wanting to make me wear pants that are so big I'll look like a clown?

When I hesitate, he shakes his baseball bat at me again.

Oh, the hell with it. I go ahead and put the pants on, and right away I can see I was right—they're way too big for me. But at least they have a drawstring that I can pull tight around my waist.

And they don't smell too bad, except for a whisper of maybe . . . mold?

The getting-me-dressed part taken care of, the baseball-bat guy ushers me out of the storage room.

I try to go back to get my shoes, but he won't let me. He uses the baseball bat to push me down a hallway and then into a large room that has rows and rows of men sitting in the same kind of gray-colored heavy-looking chairs with shiny chrome arms that I saw back in that intake building.

As soon as I enter the room, I'm hit by a bunch of really bad smells, so many smells that I'm not exactly sure what they are. The main smell is sweaty men, men that obviously haven't taken a bath in a long time. But there are other smells mixed in too, something worse. Piss? Poop? I try to figure out exactly what I'm smelling, but the smells are so powerful I feel like my sense of smell is getting overwhelmed.

The men in the chairs are all facing forward, and at first I wonder why, but then I see they're looking at a not-very-big TV set that's mounted way up next to the ceiling at the far end of the room.

Trump pushes me forward until we get to an empty chair at the end of a row that's about halfway to the front. He points at the chair and says, This is called the dayroom, and this is your chair. This is where you stay until I say otherwise. Get it? He doesn't give me a chance to answer. He grabs my shoulder and pushes me down into the chair. He leans down, close to my face and waves his hand in the general direction of the other men. He says, You see how everybody is sittin' nice and quiet watching the TV? That's what you're going to do too. You sit here in your assigned seat and keep quiet until I tell you different. Get it?

I say, Yeah, I get it, but as I keep telling you, I shouldn't be on a ward. I haven't even been evaluated by the shrink yet.

Several of the men in the rows of chairs up front turn to look back at me.

Trump points his bat at them and says, Now see what you've done. You're bothering them. I told you we like peace and quiet here in Cottage H. Now don't let me hear another peep out of you! He swings his bat at my head, and I barely have time to lean far enough away from him so his bat only strikes my shoulder.

I put up both hands and say, Okay, okay. I get it. I won't say another word.

That seems to satisfy him. He shakes his bat at the other men, and they all quickly turn back to face the front of the room.

As he leaves the room, I turn in my chair to look at the other men. Some of them glance at me, but they quickly turn away as yet another big guy comes from the back of the room and heads right toward me. The guy is not very tall, but he's wide, and his arms are so big around, his dirty white T-shirt looks like it would be sure to split open if he flexed his bulging muscles. I figure he must have had a job at some time in his life lifting a hell of a lot of real heavy stuff. Like pianos maybe.

I figure I'd better be nice to this tough-looking guy, so I give him a little wave and say, Hi. My name is—

But I don't get to finish what I was going say because he gets a grip on the back of my neck and turns my head to face the front of the room. Still holding onto the back of my neck, he leans down until his face is only inches from the side of my face. He shows me his jagged yellowed teeth, and then he growls at me . I'm not kidding, he's actually growling, like a damn pit bull dog or something, and the feel of his hand on the back of my neck is tightening, like a steel vice that's steadily getting tighter.

Just when I think he's going to break my neck in two, he finally lets go.

I move my head around a bit to make sure my neck is still working. Why the hell did he do that? Who is he and what point is he trying to make?

I watch him out of the corner of my eye as he moves away and goes to stand against the wall. He seems to be watching everybody in the room.

I figure he must be some kind of designated enforcer Trump uses to make sure everybody sits quietly and looks straight ahead.

I decide that for my own safety, I'd better sit still just like all the other men in this weird ward. I'll just sit here and keep on looking straight ahead while I try to figure out what the hell kind of place this is. The only thing I know for sure is that this is a place I really don't want to be.

"What have I got myself into this time?"

'What do you mean, Mr. Scott? Are you asking me to tell you how you ended up in this hospital?"

Oh no, not her again. She keeps on trying to convince me her reality is the real reality. But I know better. The real reality is that the cops grabbed me, and I ended up in Cottage H.

But I'm too tired to explain all that to her. Maybe I should just go to sleep. Maybe that way, I can wake up and all of this might start to make sense.

"I want to go back to my bed. I need to sleep."

"Of course, Mr. Scott. You should rest. We can pick this up again tomorrow. Maybe you will want to talk more then."

Chapter Two

I find myself sitting in a chair. Where am I? Wasn't I lying down on a couch?

Wait, now I remember. The cops stuck me in this crazy place called Cottage H. I'm sitting in the chair that Trump, the guy with the baseball bat, assigned me to, and now I know his enforcer guy will just about break the back of my neck if I try to move or even talk. There's nothing to do until I can figure out a way to get out of this place. I sure wish I had a pencil and paper so I could work on my book about the robots taking over.

Actually, now that I think about it, I don't need a pencil and paper. I can think through the story in my head and write it down later. That'll work.

Let's see. I think I left off with the hero of my story ordering one of the newfangled household robots.

Scott's new household robot didn't arrive in a box. Instead, one morning, as he was getting ready to go to work, the doorbell rang. When Scott opened the door, the robot was standing there in the hallway. At first, Scott thought it was a strange-looking pale and expressionless person that had come to visit. But then the visitor stiffly lifted its arm and held out a shiny red envelope. Scott took the envelope and found a piece of silvery metal inside that was so thin it almost felt like paper. The only thing written on the paper-like metal was the message, TO BEGIN OPERATION OF ROBOT,

PRESS HERE, and a small picture of a hand pointing at a little round target. So, this was his new household robot.

Scott pressed the middle of the target, and the robot began to speak in a flat monotone voice, its mouth barely moving: "Congratulations. I am your new My Man Friday Mr. Everything household robot from the Google Household Robot Division. My name is XR1009321A. If you need to contact the company about me for any reason, please use that designation. If you press a finger anywhere on the paper you have in your hand, my name will appear. However, you can rename me. You can give me any name you want to, and I'll remember it. If you want to give me a new name, say XR1009321A, assign new name, followed by the name you want to give me."

The robot just stood there, expressionless, staring straight ahead.

Scott cautiously pressed his finger against the metal/paper again, and the name XR1009321A magically appeared.

Then Scott realized the robot was still standing motionless in the hallway. He decided to try talk to it. He said, "Uh, do you want to come in?"

Responding with the same monotone voice, the robot said, "If you meant to give me an order, please preface it by pronouncing my name, XR1009321A. Or you can give me a new name by saying, XR1009321A, assign new name, followed by the name you want to give me."

Repeating that long string of letters and numbers all the time would be a pain, so Scott knew he had to come up with a better name. But what kind of name do you give a robot? Thinking like a logical computer programmer, he thought maybe he should just call it Robot. But what if everybody gave than name to their household robot? It might cause confusion. Well, it was his first robot, so maybe he should just call it "One." But also might be confusing if he ever had to refer to something using the number one. Maybe he could call it the number one in another language. He said, "XR1009321A, can you pronounce the number one in different languages?"

The robot immediately responded with, "English is one. Danish is en. German is eins—"

Scott said, "Stop."

"French is un. Spanish is uno. Swedish is ett. Yiddish is—"

Scott realized he had forgotten to preface his command with the robot's name. He said, "XR1009321A, stop talking."

The robot instantly stopped speaking.

"Those words are too much alike. Aren't there any number ones in some language that sound more like a name?"

The robot just stood there.

"I mean, XR1009321A, are there any number ones in any language that sound more like a human name?"

"One in Croatian is Jedan."

"That's a good one. Maybe I'll rename you Jedan."

The robot didn't respond.

"I mean, XR1009321A, I might rename you Jedan."

The robot still didn't respond.

Scott realized he has to either ask it a question or give it a command. "Okay, XR1009321A, here's a question for you. If I rename you Jedan, meaning the number one in the Croatian language, is that a good name for you?"

The robot began to speak again in its same flat mechanical voice: "The word Jedan is a popular name for boys of Jewish extraction. The name comes from the Hebrew root, Jadon, meaning grateful or thankful. It appears in the Hebrew Bible as the name of Jadon the Meronothite, one of the builders of the wall of Jerusalem."

Scott raised both hands. "Okay, I get it. Stop!"

The robot continued, "Some variants of the name are the combination of the name Jay as a short form of James or Jason or Jared with the addition with the addition of suffix aden. The name can also be used to—"

"I mean, XR1009321A, that's enough. Stop."

The robot instantly stopped talking.

My robot story feels like it's getting too complicated. I want my readers to enjoy what they're reading so they'll keep on reading until they get to the part where the robots start to take over everything. That's the important part of this book, the part that will convince them that it's really happening right now. It's the only reason I'm writing the book in the first place. I think I'll stop working on the robot-naming part and figure that out later.

> **Scott decides to quit worrying about it and just call it Robot one. "All right, XR1009321A, I rename you Robot One."**

Robot One is as good a name as any. I don't want readers to get bogged down in too much detail, unless it's interesting detail.

I hear a noise coming from the back of the room. I turn around to see what's going on. Looks like someone back there must have done something wrong. The big enforcer guy has ahold of the back of the guy's neck and is leading him out of the room. I wonder where he's taking that guy.

I decide it's none of my business, and I don't want the same thing to happen to me, so, for the moment, I'd better just sit quietly and keep working on my book.

Let's see, I was going through the process of Scott starting up his new robot. But thinking through it again, the process seems too complicated. Maybe I'd better come up with a more futuristic approach for my guy in dealing with his new robot. I think I'd better start over again, back to when he opens the door and finds his new household robot standing there. I can still use the silvery paper-like metal instructions, but I think that once he gets the robot activated and named, the robot can just tell him how to get started. I'll start over with that.

> **Scott said, all right, Robot One, now that you have a name, what do I do next?**

The robot said, "I need to become bonded to you so I respond to your commands and only to your commands. If you will allow me to engage in the formal human greeting method of shaking hands, I can detect your DNA and bond to you." The robot extends its hand.

Scott, being a really smart computer programmer, appreciated this simplified method of first association with his new robot. He extended his own hand and the robot shook it. Scott noticed how lifelike the robot's hand felt. It seemed to lack any noticeable warmth or coolness. Scott decided it must be adapting its hand to the typical temperature of a human hand.

The robot withdrew its hand and said, "Thank you. I can now identify you from all other humans, and I will respond only to your commands."

Okay, that works better. Now what's next? I guess I should have Scott figure out what else the robot can do.

Scott wasn't sure what to do next. The robot was still just standing there in the hallway, not moving at all.

Scott was suddenly worried about what his neighbors might think, so he said, "Well, why don't you come inside? Er, I mean Robot One, "Come inside my apartment."

The robot walked inside Scott's apartment in three long strides, and then it just stood there staring straight ahead.

Scott closed the door and circled around his new possession, looking it over. From the advertising materials, he knew the robot had been taught an encyclopedia's worth of facts. But other than being a repository of facts, it seemed as dumb as any other computer. Scott knew it would be a pain to have to tell it everything he wanted it to do. He thought about just sending the thing back to the manufacturer. After all, it had cost a lot of money, and there was a money-back satisfaction guarantee.

But then, Scott began to think like the smart computer programmer he was: if this robot's brain was programmed like a computer, it might be interesting to see if he could reprogram it.

But for now, he had to get to work.

"Robot One, I have to go to work. If I leave, do you uh . . . just stay here?"

This time, apparently because he had asked it a real question, the robot responded. "I will do whatever you want me to."

"Okay, Robot One, I have to leave. Do you need to sit down? Or maybe you need to plug into something to have your battery recharged."

"My battery pack is of lithium-air design. I can go more than two hundred of your hours without a recharge, and then I can plug myself into any standard household electrical outlet. It will seem like I'm asleep. However, if you want to purchase an upgrade to the latest battery design, I would be able to go more than a thousand of your hours before a recharge. Would you like me to order that upgrade?"

"Uh, no thanks. Two hundred hours is sufficient. Okay then, Robot One. How about you just stand there. I'll be back this afternoon after I get off work, and we can begin your lessons."

The robot didn't move, but it did ask a question: "Are you going to take the rapid tube to work?"

"Uh, sure. That's the way I always get to work."

"Then, on your way, you might want to stop and look at the new living room furniture on display at the newly renovated downtown Walmart furniture outlet. I noticed your furniture is rather common. Walmart's new spring collection of living room furniture is sure to impress your friends and raise your status in their eyes. All you have to do is give me the command, 'Buy Walmart Smart Furniture set number A16.' That is the furniture set most young men who are on their way up in the world want. It would be perfect for your living room."

Scott realized his new robot not only came pre-programmed with lots of facts, it also came pre-programmed with marketing spiels, like just about everything else these days. "Scott said, Uh, no thank you, Robot One. I don't spend much time here anyhow."

The robot's expression didn't change at all as it said, "I completely understand. If you change your mind later, just say, 'Buy Walmart Smart Furniture set A16,' and I will take care of it for you. I will supervise the delivery and set it up while you are at work."

Scott decided that when he began reprogramming the thing, that kind of advertising spiel would have to be one of the first things he should change. Everything came with an ad these days, and it irritated him. It was like robotic ads were now everywhere you turned. You couldn't get away from them. Even the signboards on the street talked to you very familiarly, like they were your best friend, to try to convince you to buy something. And buying something was so easy now that all you had to do was simply point your iPhone 48 at the advertising sign and say, "Buy Now!" and Amazon would deliver it by mini-drone right to your home.

Scott left the robot standing there in the middle of his living room and left for work.

I hear a murmur from the other patients, so I turn around. It's only the enforcer guy coming back into the room. The guy he took out is not with him. I wonder what that guy did wrong. Was he being delivered to Trump for some kind of punishment?

The enforcer guy looks at me, so I quickly face forward. I see out of the corner of my eye that he's gone back to standing against the wall, watching everybody.

Now what? I can't just sit here forever doing nothing. I've got to figure out how to get myself out of this weird, and apparently dangerous, Cottage H.

Then it hits me: maybe none of this is really happening. I mean I'm supposedly sitting in a really stinky room full of men, and the place is run by a big guy who calls himself Dad Trump who rules with a baseball bat. Can all that be real? And if that isn't crazy enough, there's another *really* strong guy who clamps onto the back of your neck to make sure you sit still and keep looking straight ahead. It's all too weird. I need to think this through. Maybe I'm not really in this mental hospital. Maybe I'm somewhere else. This whole thing could be a dream. Maybe I'd wake up if I pinch the skin on the back of my wrist, really hard, like I've been doing ever since I was a little kid. It's the best way to find out whether things are real or not.

"Ow!"

"What's wrong, Mr. Scott? Did something hurt you? Can I help?"

Her again. "No, you can't help. I was just testing something. But it didn't work."

"Testing something?"

"Uh, yeah, when I was a kid, sometimes I used to pinch my wrist."

"I see. And why did you do that?"

I shouldn't have told her about that trick. Now if I ever need to use it again, she'll notice. I'd better throw her off the track. "Well, it's something I used to do to take my mind off getting beat up. Like this one time after school when some mean boys surrounded me and started calling me a queer. I tried to be friendly and told them I didn't know what that word means. They laughed and said, You don't know what a queer is? That proves you are one."

"But you do now, don't you, Mr. Scott? Now you know what those boys meant by calling you that name, don't you? Were they right?"

"Sure, now I know what it means. I looked it up in the school dictionary. It means they thought I was strange. And maybe they were right, at least at that time. Back then I had more magic powers than I do now. I thought maybe that's why they were surrounding me. I figured they probably wanted me to show them a trick. So I did my invisibility trick. That way, I could accomplish two things at once, amaze them and also get away from them before I got beat up. It worked perfectly, but there's a problem with the invisibility trick: it also moves time backwards. I disappeared, and I could tell they were amazed, but then time got moved clear back to when they were calling me that name. I couldn't just keep on going invisible and then going back in time over and over, so I finally just let them beat me up, and while they were doing it, I pinched my own wrist real hard that even if I was getting hurt by them, I was also hurting myself so it didn't matter what they were doing to me."

"I see. Tell me, Mr. Scott, do you also hurt yourself in other ways?"

Uh oh, I'd better not tell her about my self-experiments. She probably won't understand that I do my self-experiments for legitimate scientific purposes. I say, "No, why do you ask?"

She doesn't answer. Instead, she starts writing something in her notebook. Is she writing something about my clever invisibility trick, or is she writing down something to report to Robot Central Command? Anyhow, it doesn't matter what she's writing. I should just stop imagining this female shrink. I know she's trying to trick me into thinking she's real. Well, she's not. I know what's real and what isn't.

To make sure my mind is really in reality mode, I force myself to focus on the details of the situation I'm in. I can very clearly feel my butt sitting in this chair, and I can very clearly smell all the other men in this room. That proves it's all real.

What else is real? Well, what about this guy who says his name is Trump? I wonder if that could really be his name. Maybe he made up that name. Or maybe I got confused and thought that's what he said his name was. Or maybe I gave him that name.

No, I wouldn't do that. I'm sure he really did say his name was Trump.

But this guy's hair is black, and it's cut short, like the kind of hair military types have.

Anyhow, whatever his name really is, he made me put on the clothes I'm wearing right now, so that proves this is all real.

And then he led me into this room. I'd better case the joint.

There seem to be about twenty chairs in this so-called day-room, all lined up in neat rows facing the front of the room. Most of the chairs are occupied, so I'm guessing there must be about fifteen guys here, all of them sitting quietly and attentively watching the TV.

And this is interesting: they're all dressed pretty much like me, in T-shirts or sweatshirts that have some kind of printed message on them. And like me, they don't have shoes on. Does it mean Dad Trump, the so-called houseparent, enjoys dressing all these patients up as if they're his children? One thing for sure, it isn't anything like the mental wards they show in movies—none of the wildly-gesticulating guys running around screaming as they chase imaginary butterflies. This place seems more like a ward for zombies.

Hey, wait a minute. Could that be what's going on here? Maybe all these so-called inmates only look like human men. Maybe they're all robots, dysfunctional robots, and this is where they store them.

But there's a problem with that idea: this is where they put me, and I'm pretty sure I'm not a robot. Maybe these inmates really *are* human, and this is where the robots store the humans they think are dysfunctional. Dysfunctional humans. That's how robots would think of crazy people. In that case, all I have to do is explain to somebody that I'm not crazy and therefore not dysfunctional. Then they'll have to let me go.

After sitting for a while, trying to not move too much, I realize that none of the others are having any problem sitting quietly.

And they're all attentively watching the TV which is showing some kind of ridiculous game show, with excited contestants dressed up in stupid clownish outfits. Why are they so interested in that TV?

Until I can get more information, I'd better just sit still and try not to gag on all the bad smells. I try to focus on the TV, but the show is so stupid, it's hopeless.

However, the big chair I'm sitting in is not all that uncomfortable, so I figure why not just sit here until I can figure out a way to get the hell out of this crazy place. Escape has to be my number one priority. After all, I don't belong here because this is obviously a place for crazy people, and like I said, I'm not crazy. Oh sure, maybe I do act a little weird when I have too much to drink, but except for that, I'm as sane as almost anybody. That reminds me, I sure could use a drink. And how long since I had a single thing to eat? Do they ever feed us? They'd have to, wouldn't they? Otherwise, we'd all die.

Oh well, better not to start thinking about that. It only makes my stomach start complaining.

What I really need to do is start making an escape plan. I look around as much as I can without turning in my chair. The guy I'm sitting next to is tall, taller I think, than anybody else in the room. Like everybody else, he seems to be very engrossed in the TV game show that's now showing a bunch of very excited people who are trying to guess the price of groceries. Hard to believe there's an actual TV show about such a dumb thing. I turn to the guy and ask him, What's this TV show all about?

He doesn't answer, and he doesn't look at me, but the guy in the chair directly in front of me, a red-headed guy, who for a change, is not all that big, turns his head slightly to the side and whispers, Don't talk to him.

I whisper back, Why not?

Because he'll kill you.

The red-headed guy said those words in such a flat voice, I can't help but wonder if he's putting me on. I say, Uh, kill me?

Yep.

Okay, Red, I'll bite. Why would he want to kill me?

My name's not Red. That's Red. He points to a guy sitting up in the front row who also has red hair. I'm Redtwo. He holds up two fingers.

I get it. Two redheads on this ward. Okay, Redtwo, like I said, why would he want to kill me?

Redtwo shrugs, still without turning his head to look directly at me. He whispers, Who knows? It's just what he does. Fried brain I guess. He points to the side of his head. Drugs probably. Too much drugs in his vein all at once I bet. We got a few of that type in here. Or maybe it's something else. Who knows?

Well, okay, Redtwo, I don't want this guy to kill me, so I guess I won't talk to . . . uh, what's his name?

Nobody knows. He came in last year. Got dumped at the front door of the main building. Out cold. And when he woke up, he started hitting anybody who came near him. So they shot him up with tranks and brought him here. He doesn't talk, so we don't know his name. We just call him Tall Mean Guy.

Got it. But you know something, Redtwo, for a guy with a fried brain, he seems mighty interested in that stupid TV game show.

Aw, he's not seeing it. The Growler parks him there in the morning after meds, and he just stares straight ahead all day.

Meds?

Meds is tranks. Tranquilizers. Powerful shit. You'll see. First thing in the morning, we get meds. Trump has a strict schedule for such things.

Okay, I get it. But you said the Growler parks him here. Who's the Growler?

You've already met the Growler. The guy who had ahold of the back of your neck.

Oh yeah, mister muscles with the vice-grip hands. The enforcer guy.

Right, but keep your voice down or you'll get to know him better than you want to.

I glance toward the Growler guy, and he's still in the same place, and thankfully, right now, he's not watching me. He's got his eye on somebody at the back of the room. I whisper to Redtwo, So, this tall mean guy next to me has a fried brain. But you don't seem to have a fried brain, Redtwo. So why are you in here?

Killed my wife.

I stare at him. Those three words about killing his wife came out in the same flat monotone whisper as all the other words he'd said. He still doesn't turn around to look at me, so I'm mostly only looking at the back of his head, but from his words, he doesn't seem especially crazy, not even as crazy as some of the guys I run into at the downtown bars. I need to know more. Okay, Redtwo, I'll bite. Why did you kill your wife?

He shrugs. Who knows? One day it just seemed like the right thing to do. I got a paring knife out of the kitchen drawer and killed her. Then I waited for the cops to come. Took two days, but eventually, when she didn't show up at the nail salon where she worked, they came.

Uh, a paring knife? Like, you mean, a small knife? I spread my finger and thumb a few inches apart to show him.

He glances back. Yeah. About like that.

Sounds pretty violent.

Yeah, I guess so. Messy. The cops wanted to know why I did it. I told them I didn't know, and I told the judge the same thing, so that judge sent me here. Everybody on this ward is like me. Did something violent.

Violent? I look around at the men staring at the TV. None of them seem the slightest bit violent.

Redtwo whispers, Yep. Real violent. Didn't they tell you? Cottage H is a special ward for violent men. It's always locked up tight. No visitors allowed. Even the doctors are scared to come in here. But it's not as violent as they say, long as you don't get on wrong side of anybody.

So, you'll tell me if I'm about to get on your wrong side, won't you? I grin to let him know I'm making a joke.

He turns his head just enough to look at me out of the corner of his eye. You're not my wife, are you?

I'm not sure if it was a real question, but I decide to play it safe. No, Redtwo, I'm not. My name's . . . uh, Scotty. For some reason, I'd almost slipped and told him my real name, but luckily I caught myself in time.

"No, really, my name actually is Scotty."

"Yes, I was told you like to go by that name."

What the hell? I wasn't talking to her, was I? I'd better pay attention. The robots could be listening.

"Mr. Scott? Are you back with me?"

Careful now, don't let her know I'm onto her. "Uh, sure. Where else would I be?"

"Well, sometimes you . . . Never mind. You were telling me about your childhood. Would you like to continue?"

I was? What was I telling her? I hope I wasn't letting slip any of my secrets.

"Mr. Scott?"

"Oh, right. Uh, what was I telling you?"

"You were telling me some boys at your school used to call you names and attack you."

"I was? Uh, I mean, right, I was. Well, there was this one time in high school when I was the star of the cross country running team. Nobody could beat me, so one day when we were training by running in this park, around a lake, the other boys on the team hid and waited for me to come along. They blocked the path and ganged up on me and pushed me into the lake. Then they got some long sticks and kept on jabbing me with them to make sure I couldn't get out of the water. I was pretty sure I was going to drown. In fact, I'm pretty sure I did drown."

"Well now, Mr. Scott, if you drowned, how could you be here now talking to me?"

"Oh, that. Well, you see it's like this. I actually have many different forms."

"Different forms? Tell me about that?"

Hmm, no matter what I say, she always comes back at me with a question. Is that what all shrinks do, or is there another reason for her constant questioning? It's making me more and suspicious that she may be working for the robots. Maybe they found out about my book and they started investigating me, and eventually they learned about my superpowers. That got them interested in me, so they got their cops to lock me up in this place so they can learn more about me. I never should have told her about my ability to take on different forms. And I absolutely can't tell her the truth about how when I was a kid I could shape-shift into different people.

"Mr. Scott? Are you still with me?"

"Uh, sure. I'm right here. Where else would I be?"

"You were telling me about the time some mean boys pushed you into a lake."

"Oh, right. Well, eventually they got tired of tormenting me, and they left."

"So, you didn't drown?"

"Naw. If I'd of drowned I couldn't be here now talking to you, could I?"

"No, of course not. But you said you were pretty sure you did drown. Why did you tell me that? Do you sometimes wish you were dead?"

"No, sometimes I really do die, but then I always change my mind and come back to life. Maybe one of these days I'll just stay dead and that will be the end of it. Unless maybe when we die, we don't actually stay dead. One time when I died, I was sure that this time I was really dead, but things went right on as if nothing had happened at all. Ever since then, I've been pretty sure that's what heaven really is. It's not like religious people think, that you float up into the sky and get to sit on a cloud with God and the angels. No, when you die, you do get to go to a kind of heaven, but it's actually just another form of your life, with everything going on the same as it was—the same world with the same people and the same rules of physics and everything.

The physicists proved it. They taught me about that when I was at that college. They call it the law of infinite possibilities. They proved that if everything is infinite, sooner or later, there'll be an exact copy of our earth with everything the same. So, now I know that's what heaven is. We just get transported to another version of the same thing. It feels the same, but it's actually just an exact copy of our life on another earth that's also the same."

"Well, Mr. Scott, that is certainly an interesting theory. How long have you had this belief?"

So she's calling it a belief. Here I go to all the trouble to explain it all to her, and she just thinks it's only my belief. Well the hell with her. See if I bother to explain things to her anymore.

I lean forward to ask Redtwo more questions, but before I can ask him anything else, I again feel the vice on the back of my neck. The Growler pulls me back into my chair and whispers into my ear, No talk!

So the Growler can talk. I thought maybe he was some new kind of non-talking robot. But maybe since he's just the enforcer robot, they made him so he can only say a few words at a time.

When he finally lets loose of my neck, I turn my head back and forth a few times to make sure it's still working. I wonder how many times my poor neck will be able to take his vice-like grip.

The Growler goes back to his observation place standing against the wall. He's still staring at me, like he's almost daring me to talk again. Why don't they want us patients to talk to each other? Why should the robots care if we talk?

I rub the back of my neck. It still hurts. I can see why the place is so quiet. But don't think I can take not being allowed to talk. If I can't at least talk to Redtwo, maybe I really will go crazy and end up a zombie, like the other men in this so-called Cottage H.

If only I was sitting right next to Redtwo. We could talk in a whisper, and the Growler would never know.

Hmm. That gives me an idea. I might be able to kill two birds with one stone, as they say. If my plan works, I can find out how violent these guys really are and end up sitting next to Redtwo so we can talk more.

The guy in the chair next to Redtwo is kind of tough looking. Tall and lanky, the kind of guy I've run into in bars. I've learned (the hard way) they are good fighters. I'll name him Tough Lanky Guy.

I turn to look at the Tall Mean Guy sitting next to me. Redtwo says nobody can talk to him because he'll attack. Maybe I can use that to get what I want.

I wait until the Growler heads to the other side of the room to do his vice-on-the-back-of-the-neck thing on somebody over there, then I lean forward and smack Tough Lanky Guy on the back of his head.

Tough Lanky Guy turns around. He looks angry.

I point to Tall Mean Guy.

Tough Lanky Guy reaches back and punches Tall Mean Guy in the chest.

Tall Mean Guy jumps up and picks up his chair and holds it over his head.

I can't believe what my eyes are seeing: it's hard to believe any human being could actually be strong enough to lift one of those heavy chairs, let alone have the strength to hold it over his head.

After a few seconds of mutual staring, Tall Mean Guy brings the heavy chair down on top of Tough Lanky Guy's head.

Tough Lanky Guy goes down in a heap. He's not moving,

Oh no, I hope my little experiment hasn't killed the guy.

I look back to see what the Growler is going to do about this. For some reason, he's left the room.

Tall Mean Guy carefully puts his chair back in place, exactly where it was before, and sits back down on it. He goes back to staring straight ahead.

Trump comes running into the room brandishing his baseball bat. The Growler is right behind him.

Trump yells, All right, what the hell is going on in here?

First time I've heard Trump yell, and he's red in the face.

I jump up and point to Tall Mean Guy. He's still sitting quietly, still staring straight ahead.

I say, He hit that guy with his chair. He just picked up his chair and brought it down on that poor guy's head.

Trump shakes his head, like he's disgusted. He says, Shit, not again. He points at me. You, new guy. Help the Growler drag him back to the dorm.

The Growler gets ahold of poor out-cold Tough Lanky Guy under the armpits and starts dragging him toward the open doorway at the back of the room. I can barely keep up, so I just grab onto Tough Lanky Guy's pant legs and pretend to be helping. We go through the doorway into a wide hallway with nothing in it except a beat-up metal desk. It must be Trump's desk. We go through another doorway that leads into a large room with rows and rows of beds that are right next to each other. This must be the dormitory. I try to imagine sleeping here all night with violent men all around me. If these men are as violent as Redtwo says, how does Trump, or the Growler, keep them from killing each other in the darkness?

I help the Growler toss Tough Lanky Guy onto what I assume is his assigned bed. He's still out cold, but he does groan a little. Thank goodness, he's not dead.

The Growler gets ahold of my elbow and leads me back to the dayroom where Boss Trump is pacing back and forth, pointing his baseball bat at the men, one after the other. He seems nervous. Is he nervous because the Growler wasn't there to protect him from all these violent men?

I go to sit in Tough Lanky Guy's chair, the chair next to Redtwo. I act like it's my normal place. I wait for the vice on the back of my neck.

But it never comes.

I look around. Trump is at the back of the room talking to the Growler.

Redtwo whispers to me, That was mean of you.

I know Redtwo is right; I shouldn't have done something to get Tough Lanky Guy hurt, but it got me what I wanted. What I needed. I sit up straight and whisper to Redtwo out of the side of my mouth, I had to get myself into a chair where I have somebody to talk to. Otherwise, I really would go crazy.

So, you don't think you belong here?

I don't because I'm not crazy. And I'm not violent either.

Redtwo makes a sort of Hmft sound.

Well, no matter what he thinks, I'm not crazy. Really I'm not. I may have trouble knowing what is real sometimes, but who can be sure of that?

Anyhow, my little test did confirm something I needed to know: the men on this ward really are violent, and they can be easily provoked. I'll have to watch my step until I can see a shrink and get myself out of here.

I lean a little closer to Redtwo so I can whisper to him without the Growler hearing. I say, A question, Redtwo. Does that Growler guy just stand there against that wall watching us all day long?

Yeah, pretty much. He does whatever Trump tells him to do, but his main job is keeping us all in line.

I say, So he works for Trump. He's an employee of this place?

Naw. He doesn't exactly work for Trump. Like you said, he's Trump's enforcer. But he's actually a patient, like the rest of us. I don't know how he got to be Trump's enforcer. Happened before my time here.

Now I'm getting it. But is Trump a robot? Probably not. If he was a robot, he probably wouldn't need to anybody like the Growler guy as his enforcer. Robots are stronger than anybody, even stronger than a strong guy like the Growler. And Trump seems to have plenty of muscles of his own. But maybe his kind of robot doesn't like to get his hands dirty, so to speak.

I turn to look at the Growler guy. He's still standing against the wall, arms folded, staring at me.

Redtwo whispers, Don't look at him.

I whisper back, Why? Is he like Tall Mean Guy? Will he kill me if I get on his wrong side.

Redtwo shrugs and says, It's possible. Believe me, you don't want to test him.

I'm beginning to think whispering in a flat voice and shrugging are Redtwo's main modes of communication. I need to know more, but decide to hold off asking him questions for a bit. Wouldn't want him to get upset with me and decide it might be a good idea to kill me.

I go back to trying to figure all this out. How can any of this be real? For example, this guy who calls himself Redtwo says this place is for the most violent patients. So why did they send me here? Because they think I broke their door? Or did that cop write something on my admittance form that said I was a violent bar fighter? Me, violent? Hey, I'm the least violent guy on the planet. I'm not kidding. I never hit anybody in my entire life, not even when I was a kid.

"I was the quiet kid in the schoolyard, the one who stayed in the shadows so I didn't get beat up."

"Is that right, Mr. Scott? You say someone beat you up when you were a child? I'm sorry to hear that. Would you like to talk about it?"

"Well, it was a long time ago, but the main thing I remember about going to that school was that I used to get beat up a lot by this one particular bully, the biggest schoolyard bully they had there. So I tried to stay out of his way. Unfortunately, that usually didn't work. He beat me up so often, I kind of got used to it. Then one day, I was sitting in the grass at recess watching the other kids play kickball when he noticed me and must have decided too many days had elapsed since the last time he'd beat me up. He came over and started hitting me. I did my usual thing: turn onto my side, pull my legs up, cover my face with my hands, wait for him to get tired of hitting and kicking me. But on that day, the absurdity of the situation—skinny little me getting beat up once again by big fat bully—got to me. I started laughing. I guess my laughing made him mad 'cause he started hitting me even harder. That seemed even more absurd to me. What was his point? Didn't he ever get bored with hitting skinny little kids like me? At that moment, he seemed like some kind of cartoon character, and that got me to laughing even harder. And then he stopped. He just stood there, fists still up and ready, staring down at me. I peeked through my fingers to see why he had stopped. What I saw surprised me: his eyes seemed confused, maybe even a little scared. My laughing had confused him. He couldn't figure out why I wasn't crying and begging for mercy, like I usually did. Believe it or not, he helped me up, and after that day, he didn't beat me up anymore. In fact, he tried to make friends with me. That same day, after school, he caught up with me and walked all the way home with me. I kept my mouth shut and looked down as we walked, but he was cheerful and he never stopped talking. He talked about this and that as if we'd been pals forever. Every day after that—at least on the days when he wasn't staying after school to beat somebody up—he always walked home with me. He'd ramble on, bragging about all the kids he'd beat up that day, and about the girls he'd hit on. Trouble was, he couldn't seem to get anywhere with those girls. It seemed to really bother him that those girls didn't get that they should like him for heroically beating up the other kids. One day, I couldn't keep my mouth shut any longer, so I quietly suggested that maybe those girls didn't like the fact that he was beating up kids that were smaller than him. He stopped dead in his tracks and stood there staring at me. But then he recovered, and we went back to walking. It was clear that he couldn't quite grasp what I meant: if what I had said was true, then what would be the point of beating kids up? At that moment, I realized that he wasn't just a big fat bully that liked to beat up on little kids; he was actually doing it for a real purpose: to get girls to like him. He was actually being logical. Despite all appearances, he was actually a reasonable, thoughtful human being. His reasoning maybe have been flawed, but whose isn't? It was a lesson I never forgot: people really do have reasons for what they do, no matter how crazy their actions might seem.

After that, we remained friends, if you'd call walking home together and him doing all the talking is being friends. But he never mentioned girls to me again. Once we got out of that school and went to high school, he didn't last long. He soon ran into bigger and tougher bullies there, so he left school, lied about his age, and got them to accept him into the United States Army. The word around school was that he got sent to the latest U.S. war of invasion somewhere over there and killed a lot of the enemy before they killed him back."

"I see. Well, I appreciate you sharing that memory with me, Mr. Scott. I was told you do actually sometimes talk, and you can be quite articulate. It seems they were right. In fact, I'd like to compliment you on your ability to tell a story. Quite vividly done."

She's complimenting me on my story? Why? What is she up to? I'd better not let her get me distracted. I should make sure I hang onto the delicate thread of the real reality, I can't let it slip through my fingers, or I'll get lost again, like before.

I need to explain to somebody that I don't belong on this ward for violent men. There's been some kind of mistake made. Me, violent? I'm not only not likely to kill anybody, I don't even want to hit anybody. But who can I explain that to? Redtwo warned me not to talk to anybody.

But maybe what Redtwo is telling me isn't true. Lately, I've been having a little bit of trouble determining what is true and not true, and ending up in this weird Cottage H isn't helping. Maybe I should just not believe him. Not believing people is something I do well.

Of course, not believing people sometimes gets me beat up. Since I was a kid, I've had a tendency to test what is seen by others as truth, and sometimes my testing them gets them mad at me. But it's just the way it is. I can't help it if I'm the only one who knows how things really are. I'm only trying to help them by pointing out their false beliefs. Problem is, they often *really* want to believe whatever it is they believe. My straightening them out upsets them, so they shoot the messenger. That is, they beat me up so they don't have to hear the truth anymore.

And now, given my truth-seeking need, I naturally want to know if Redtwo is actually telling me the truth. He claims the reason all the sleepy-eyed men on this ward are all sitting quietly and looking straight forward in the general direction of the TV is because of the so-called meds. But maybe that's not the real reason. They look a lot like mind-controlled robots, so maybe Robot Central Command hired Trump to make troublesome humans be more robot like.

That's a new thought. If the robots can't make themselves into humans, maybe they're trying to make us humans be more like them. Back when the robots started changing their skin coverings so they would look more like us humans, it was only because they wanted us humans to like them. Eventually, they got so good at looking and acting like humans, I was the only one who could tell which ones were the real humans and which ones were the robots. It wasn't long before I figured out that robots were starting to appear all over the place within our society, acting like they were humans. I could tell they were robots because of their unblinking eyes. Unfortunately, they fixed that by adjusting their own programs to make their eyes blink on a pseudo-random schedule. Since then, they've also made other improvements, so now it's getting harder and harder to tell which ones are the real humans and which ones are the robots.

I look around the room. All the men in this so-called day-room look human, but they do seem mindless. They might be robots. But maybe it's like Redtwo said, the meds make them act that way. If so, those meds must be really powerful. I bet the robots invented those drugs specifically to make violent men sit real quiet and act like zombies.

I start to ask Redtwo about that, but then I see the Growler coming, so I sit back and look straight ahead.

Luckily, this time the Growler goes right past us and heads all the way up to the front row.

He jerks a thin little guy up out of his chair and leads him out of the room by holding onto the back of his neck.

I lean closer to Redtwo and whisper, What did that little guy do? Where is the Growler taking him?

Redtwo continues to look straight ahead as he whispers, That's Queer Tommy. He got put in here for being a homo. Trump sometimes parks him under his desk so he can get off while he looks at his dirty picture books.

I stare at Redtwo. Is he making some kind of sick joke? The guy in charge of a ward full of mental patients would use a patient sexually? I whisper, You're kidding, right?

Redtwo says, Nope. Watch and learn. You'll see how things work here in Cottage H.

So, Trump is gay?

Redtwo shakes his head. Naw, he brings in girls sometimes too. Depends on how he feels that day.

Soon, the Growler is back. He takes up his usual station standing against the wall, keeping close watch on us.

I can hardly believe Redtwo is telling me the truth. I whisper to him, Jesus, Redtwo, what the hell kind of place is this?

He lets out a low chuckle and whispers, Hell is right. Cottage H. H is for hell. You'll see.

His little laugh reminds me of the laugh I heard Barefoot Billy let out when that intake robot in the dark suit told the guards to take me to Cottage H. Does everybody in this institution know about Cottage H? Has it been designated as some kind of punishment ward where Trump is given free reign to do whatever he wants to us patients? I whisper to Redtwo, So, are there other wards like this?

Nope, he says.

Well, I say, tell me about more about this Cottage H. Like, what's the daily schedule?

He says, Get up at dawn. Line up for meds. Watch TV. Eat breakfast. Watch TV. Lunch in the afternoon. Sit in these chairs all day and watch TV. Go to bed.

That's it?

Pretty much. Except for Trump's morning card game.

Card game?

Yeah. Trump loves his little daily card game. He gets three or four of us patients to play it with him every day.

I look around at the zombie-like men and try to imagine any of them being capable of playing a card game.

But thinking about it, maybe if I can get myself into that game, I won't turn into a zombie like all these other guys. I whisper to Redtwo, How does he decide who gets to play? Could I get in his game?

You'll be in it today. Whenever a new guy comes onto the ward, Trump always tests him out with his card game.

Okay, how do you play this game?

Nuthin' to it. It's just a silly kid's game. You'll pick it up. Besides, you don't really need to know how to play. You just let Trump win.

Okay, I get it. But you mentioned breakfast. When is that? I can't remember when I ate last.

He says, You're in luck. You got here in time for breakfast.

Breakfast? Really? This late? I'm not exactly sure what time it is, but it's been daylight outside for hours. At least I think so.

Yeah. Trump makes us wait until the meds kick in good before he lets us go to the dining room to eat. That way, nobody makes any trouble.

There's that meds term again. Everything in this place seems to revolve around meds. Glad they didn't give me any when I got here. Guess it means they know I'm not really crazy.

I suddenly realize I have to pee. In fact, I have to pee real bad. Despite all the booze I drank last night, I don't remember peeing since then. Did I pee in my pants somewhere along the line? That thought again makes me remember that hard plastic back seat in the police car, the seat the cops talked about hosing out when they got back to the station. Did I pee my pants in that back seat? Now that I think about it, why can't I remember more about that car ride?

I whisper to Redtwo, What do you all do if you have to pee?

He whispers back, Hey, man, can't you smell it? Most of the men on this ward are so tranked up they just go in their pants.

He's right. Now I do recognize one of the main bad smells I've been smelling ever since I got here. Human urine. Well, at least it tells me this is the real reality. Smells are real.

I suddenly realize what the other bad smell I've been smelling is: poop. Some of these patients must also be pooping in their pants. I lean closer to Redtwo. Are you saying I have to do it in my pants?

He chuckles. Naw. Not unless you're one of the cats. Cats get a towel stuffed into their pants so they can just let it go.

Cats?

Catatonics. Like the guy sitting right next to you. Can't you smell him?

I turn to look at the guy. And now I really can smell him. He smells strongly of piss and poop. But he's so small and so slumped down in his chair, I hardly even noticed him even though he's been sitting right next to me. How could I have not noticed him? It's like he just suddenly appeared when Redtwo mentioned him. Must be because he's so unbelievably thin, like nothing more than a skeleton with a bit of skin stretched over. And he's very pale. No, not pale, more like . . . gray. Like dead-person gray. Could he actually be dead and still be sitting in a chair right next to me? I touch his arm. He doesn't react. With one finger, I jab his arm, harder. He pulls his arm away, but it happens in a way that almost looks automatic, as if it's one of those autonomic responses I learned about when I was at Harvard College.

I turn back to Redtwo and whisper, Jesus, he almost looks dead.

As usual, Redtwo just shrugs, and then says, Yeah. Probably will be soon. The cats don't last long on this ward because we can't get them to eat anything. I've tried with this one, but Cat-four won't eat.

That's his name? Catfour? So does that mean there are three other catatonics on this ward?

Used to be. They died.

Three of them died?

Yep.

Really? Can't we do anything to help this one?

You can try. Catfour won't get up to go to the dining room. If we try to drag him, he fights us. I got ahold of an apple one time. I tried to give some of it to him, but he wouldn't eat it. Not even if I stuck pieces of it into his mouth. He just let it sit there on top of his tongue. Never did swallow it. I've been able to drag him to the toilet room a few times. He fought me, but a few times I've been able to get water out of the tap and pour a bit of it into his mouth. I make him swallow some water whenever I can so he doesn't die of thirst. But actually, I don't know how he's hung on this long.

I stare at the poor guy. Maybe I can find a way to help him. But in the meantime, I still need to pee, real bad. I turn back to Redtwo. So, you said we're allowed to go pee. How do I do that?

Boss Trump doesn't like the mess, so all you gotta do is raise your hand and ask permission to go to the toilet room. Here, I'll show you. He raises his hand real high, waving it at the Growler. Gotta take a leak, boss.

The Growler grunts and does the slightest bit of a nod.

Redtwo gets up and heads through a door at the front of the room. I figure that door must lead to the restroom.

Even though I'm the new guy on the ward, I decide to take a chance and try the same thing. I raise my hand and say, Gotta pee, boss.

The Growler does the same kind of grunt and nod he'd done when Redtwo asked. Then he goes back to scanning the room, watching everybody.

I hope his grunt and nod means I can go without getting his vice grip on the back of my neck again. I get up and head for the same door Redtwo disappeared through.

I make it out of the dayroom without the Growler stopping me or any of the other patients killing me. The door leads to a short hallway and halfway along it, I see an open doorway that leads out onto a screened-in porch. Is it a possible way to sneak off of this ward? I peek through the doorway, and I'm disappointed to see that the heavy mesh screens are way too thick to cut through, even if I had some kind of tool to do it.

I hear somebody talking out there on the screened-in porch, so I step out. A big black guy is pacing back and forth, and he's waving his hands in the air and ranting about something. I listen to him long enough to figure out his talking is cussing. He's cussing somebody out. Squeezed in between strings of other swear words, I hear the words You bitch and You Goddam whore.

What the hell? How can this big black guy be out there on a screened-in porch pacing and cursing while all the other patients back in the dayroom and are being forced to sit quietly. How can this guy get away with that when the rest of us can't even whisper without the Growler trying to break the back of our necks?

I go on back into the hallway and go on to the restroom. It's a long, high-ceiling room, and one whole wall is lined with old-fashioned tall urinals. The opposite wall is lined with ancient-looking yellowed toilets. There are no dividers between the urinals and no stalls around the toilets, so if you're shy about others watching you do your business, this is obviously the wrong place for you. But actually, compared to some of the sleazy bars I've been in downtown, this old-looking restroom seems fairly clean.

I go to the urinal next to Redtwo and finally get to pee.

Redtwo is looking me over, and that means I can finally get a better look at him. He's actually a kind of handsome guy with a long nose and a jutting chin. His very white skin, which contrasts with his red hair, tells me it's been quite a while since he's seen sunlight. He's wearing a dark sweatshirt with what used to be words on the front of his shirt. The words are faded, but I'm pretty sure the first word ended in Y. Another word is maybe DATE, but who knows? Doesn't matter. I've got to figure out a way to escape this crazy place, and maybe Redtwo can help.

He glances down at my male part and does something in his throat that might have been a chuckle. If he's chuckling at the size of my protuberance, I don't appreciate it very much, but at least it proves he's not a robot.

When Redtwo is finished peeing, he doesn't move, so when I'm done, I decide to also stay where I am. I ask him who that scary big black guy out there in the screened-in porch is, and why is he ranting all those cuss words.

He glances in that direction and does a dismissive wave with his hand. Don't worry about him. That's just the Big Black Cusser. He's the least dangerous person on this ward. Gentle as a baby. He's not mad at anybody except his wife. That's who he's cussing out. If you listen to him for a while, you can figure out she's the one who put him in here.

I say, They let him go on like that all day while everybody else has to sit quietly in front of the TV?

Well, they can't stop him. Tranks don't seem to have any effect on him, so they let him stay out there on the porch and cuss all he wants. Any other questions?

Yeah, lots. Like if that Growler guy really is a patient, like you said, why does he do whatever Trump tells him to?

Redtwo glances toward the door and lowers his voice. I don't know what the Growler's deal is. I mean I don't know what got him put in here. But he does whatever Trump tells him to do 'cause he's scared of meds. You wouldn't think a tough guy like the Growler would be scared of anything, but for some reason he's scared of meds, and Trump is the one who controls the meds.

So that's all the Growler does? Watch us?

Yeah, except, sometimes he goes off ward to do Trump's errands. Like I said before, he sometimes goes out to get a girl Trump.

Really? The Growler gets girls for Trump?

Yeah. Trump takes 'em into his apartment for a while. The Growler is in charge of us until he's done with 'em. Then, the Growler takes the girl back to her ward.

To her ward? You mean the girls are patients?

Yeah, and they're real young. Just kids, actually.

Redtwo is telling me these things in his usual flat, matter-of-fact way, but I can hardly believe what he's saying. How can Trump get away with stuff like that? Aren't the robots that run this institution aware that that kind of thing is going on? I say, Uh, how long has that kind of thing been going on?

Redtwo does his usual shrug and says, For a long time, I think. As long as I've been on this ward, at least. And the Growler sometimes goes out to get other stuff for Trump. I'm not sure what. He brings the stuff back in paper bags, and Trump hides it in his desk.

I'm trying to digest what Redtwo is telling me, but now I'm really getting worried. It's like this Trump guy can get away with anything.

But it means Trump is probably not a robot. What would a robot want with young human girls? Unless he's experimenting on them or something.

But then I think of another question. You said Trump takes them to his apartment? Does that mean he lives here? All the time?

Right. That's the houseparent model they use in this joint. The houseparents are usually a husband and wife team, but in Cottage H, it's only Trump. He rules this ward with an iron hand, with the help of the Growler of course. He looks toward the door and says, Any more questions? We'd better be heading back to our chairs.

My mind is reeling from all the weird stuff Redtwo is telling me, and I need time to think all this through. But I need to know more if I'm going to find a way out of this crazy place. I say, Uh, you keep mentioning the meds. What's that all about?

Meds is medicine. Tranks, like I said. That's Trump's main thing to control us. Everybody gets meds.

Everybody?

Yep, everybody. And if anybody gets out of line and makes trouble, they get more meds. You'll see tomorrow morning. Every morning, Trump lines us all up and decides who needs what meds. Maybe it's based on how they acted the day before, or maybe it's based on something in Trump's head. Whatever, it's all about control. Trump wants everybody to just sit in their assigned chair and stare straight ahead all day long. If they don't, they get more meds.

So, is he some kind of doctor? A doctor with a baseball bat?

Redtwo laughs. He's no doctor. Far from it. He never even finished high school. At least that's what he says. Brags about it during his daily card game. Says he quit high school and went straight into the Army. Says the Army taught him everything he needs to know about life.

So where do the meds come from?

Beats me. Some little barefoot guy named Billy brings them in at night. In big jars. Trump puts 'em in the med closet, and in the morning he decides who needs what.

Amazing, I say. Is this whole place run like that? The other wards, I mean?

Naw. The other wards are all open.

Open?

Open means you can walk right out the door and leave if you want to.

I say, I saw a lot of other cottages like this one when they brought me in. Do you know how many patients they have in this place?

Hundreds, I think. Maybe thousands.

That amazes me. I say, If the other wards are open, why do the patients stay?

Redtwo shrugs. Guess they got nowhere else to go. It's my theory that this entire hospital is one big warehouse for people who got nowhere else to go.

Well, I've got other places to go, so will they let me leave? Eventually, I mean.

Redtwo makes a sort of snort sound. Not a chance. Once they put you in Cottage H, you're here to stay. Don't forget, H stands for Hell, and once you're in Hell, you don't get out.

That's such a scary thought, I want to ask Redtwo more questions, like hasn't anybody ever gotten out, but the Growler appears at the restroom door and yells, Hey!

Redtwo pulls his sweatpants up real quick, grabs a quick drink of water out of the sink tap, and then hurries toward the door.

I do the same and follow in Redtwo's footsteps. For some reason, Redtwo is walking very slow and shuffling his feet. Is that what the meds do to you? But he wasn't walking like that before.

The Growler growls at us as we squeeze past him.

Back in our chairs, I think through what I've learned so far. Redtwo told me such amazing stuff, my mind is reeling as I try to make sense of it all. He seems to know everything that goes on in Cottage H. He even knows what Trump does. But he's stuck in his chair all day, just like I am, so how did he learn all that stuff? It's almost like he's just making it up, like the way I used to make up stuff when I was a kid.

But no, he must be telling me the truth. Why would he make up something crazy like that?

Well, I don't want to think about that right now. I need to keep my focus on what I've learned so far about this weird Cottage H. I guess the main thing I've learned is that Trump lives here all the time, and that he gives everybody enough meds to make them sit still in these chairs and stare straight ahead all day.

But why would the robots have created a place like this? Robots do what they're programmed to do, so maybe Robot Central Command has programmed them to try to program us humans to be like them. Maybe this Cottage H is a place to do controlled experiments on mental patients to learn how to turn them into robot-like zombies.

But why only this one cottage? Redtwo said the other wards were open, meaning the patients can leave. But they don't. Are those other wards where the robots keep the humans that are already fully under their control?

"Hey, maybe I should put that in my book."

"You book, Mr. Scott? Are you referring to the book you say you are planning to write? The book about robots?"

"Uh, yes. Sorry, I was thinking out loud."

"I see. Do you do that often? Think out loud, I mean. And do you sometimes feel there is somebody listening to your words, somebody eavesdropping on you?"

Another one of her weird questions. Where is she going with this? I'd better not let on that I know the robots really are listening to all of us all of the time using their satellite-controlled listening devices. "Uh, no. I was just thinking through something. When you're trying to work through something, sometimes it helps to say it out loud. Don't you ever do that?"

"I see. Certainly we all do have our unique ways of working through problems. Do you feel you have a lot of problems?"

I shake my head to make sure she knows she's not going to be able to lead me down that path. "No, not many problems. No more than anybody else. Uh, don't you want to ask me anything about my childhood?"

"Of course, Mr. Scott. I'm always interested in anything you can tell me about your formative childhood experiences. Were you thinking about something in particular?"

"Well, I was going to tell you about the time I did something heroic. But if you don't want to hear it."

"No, please go on. I'm always interested in your stories."

"Well, okay. There was this one time when I was in school and a little boy fell out of his desk right next to me and started flopping around on the floor. The other kids laughed at him and said, Here goes the Flopper, flopping around like a fish again. The poor kid was having some kind of seizure, and all the other kids could do was make fun of him. But not me. I sat down on the floor next to him and put my hands under his head to keep him from banging it on the floor. He was banging his head so hard it hurt my hands, but I kept them under his head until he finally slowed down and then stopped. The teacher thanked me for trying to help the boy, and then she took him to the school nurse. Of course, while she was gone, the mean boys started making fun of me, saying it made sense, the Flopper and the weird kid, two of a kind."

"That was very nice of you to help that boy, Mr. Scott. Were you always kind when you were young?"

"I sure was. You want to know the kindest thing I did when I was a kid?"

"Yes, I would like that."

"The kindest thing I did when I was that age was not using my superpowers to punish the boys that were mean to me. In fact, I made it a rule never to use my superpowers for anything but good."

"Can you tell me more about those superpowers. Mr. Scott?"

I shake my head again. "No sorry. That will have to remain my secret. It's a rule."

"Well, maybe you could at least tell me how you learned about your special powers."

"I'm afraid all I can tell you is that I was special. As a child, I mean. I was a quick study. I had hundreds of comic books about superheroes, and I studied them at night in my bed. I made a tent out of my sheets and got a little flashlight under there so I could read them over and over again until I learned how to duplicate all their superpower tricks. But I didn't let on to anybody. Like I said, I only used my superpowers for good, never for evil."

"I see. Did you imagine you were the superheroes in those comic books?"

She doesn't get it at all. You don't *become* the superheroes, you just learn their tricks. Why do I bother even talking to her?

I'm still wondering why the robots created a place like Cottage H when the Growler comes to the end of our row and signals for me to come with him. Not wanting the vice on the back of my neck, I quickly stand up. Then he points to Redtwo who also stands up.

What does he want with the two of us? Did Trump see us talking together? Is the Growler taking us to him for some kind of punishment?

The Growler leads us toward the back of the room where I see a card table has been set up. It's surrounded by five chairs.

I lean closer to Redtwo and whisper, What's up?

He whispers back, The card game.

Oh, that's right. You told me about that. Will Trump tell us how to play?

No. Just act dumb, and you'll do fine.

Growler sits us down and goes to get two other patients.

Redtwo and the other two patients sit quietly and stare straight ahead, so I do the same. Luckily, I'm sitting to Redtwo's left, so if this card game is anything like the card games my family played when I was a kid, I'll be able to watch what he does before it's my turn to act.

Trump arrives, all smiles. He sits down and places a deck of cards and a notepad on the table. He parks his baseball bat against the wall behind his chair and looks around at each of us. Well, boys, how're ya'll doin' today?

Redtwo says, Fine, but nobody else responds. I decide not to respond either. I don't know what he's up to, but I'm not going to play Trump's little being friendly game. I'm not going to be here in this so-called Cottage H for long anyhow.

And how about you, New Guy? Settling in?

He's looking at me, waiting for me to respond. Does he want me to say something pleasant? Well, the hell with that. I don't feel pleasant about him. His way of dealing with me when I arrived in this place was to hit me with his baseball bat. So why is he acting so nice now?

Trump nods. Good, good. Glad to hear it. He chuckles.

I glance at Redtwo, but he's still staring straight ahead.

I turn to look at the Growler. He's gone back to his usual watching station against the wall. He keeping his eyes on the patients in the chairs and doesn't seem to be paying any attention to Trump's card game.

I turn back to the game and see that Trump is writing something on the top of his notebook. Is he actually going to keep score?

He begins to shuffle the cards, humming to himself. He actually seems happy. This stupid card game must be the highlight of his day.

He deals out cards, seven to each of us, and then he places the deck in the middle of the table and turns over a card. It's the ten of clubs.

I have no idea how the game is played, but luckily it's not my turn. Apparently, it's the turn of the first guy that's sitting to Trump's left, a little guy that seems to have a permanent scared look on his face. He picks up his cards and holds them up close. But he doesn't do anything else.

Trump pulls down the guy's cards so he can look at them and says, You don't have any clubs, Shrimp. You have to draw a card.

So the little guy's name is Shrimp. Does Trump give everybody a nickname?

Shrimp doesn't move. He just continues to stare straight ahead. Is he that much under the influence of those meds Redtwo was telling me about, or is he just too scared to act?

Trump draws a card off of the top of the deck and looks at it. Well, Shrimp, good draw. It's the jack of clubs. Lucky you. He places the card, face up, on top of the seven of clubs.

Next, it's Redtwo's turn. He pulls a card out of his hand. It's the Jack of diamonds. He places it on top of the jack of clubs.

Okay, I get it. The point of this card game must be that you either have to match the suit of the card that's showing or have a card of the same denomination, and you put it down until you get rid of all your cards. Simple game. Pointless and mindless, but it's better than sitting still staring at the stupid TV. Besides, it gives me a chance to study Trump, so I decide to play along. I have the ten of diamonds, so I place it on top of the jack of diamonds.

Trump seems surprised. He says, So, New Guy, you do know how the game goes. This is gonna be fun.

The guy to my left is thin and almost as short as the Shrimp, and he doesn't look very healthy. He is holding his seven cards in his hand, but he doesn't seem to realize it's his turn to play.

Trump chuckles and reaches over to look at the guy's cards. Aw, too bad, Flopper, he says. Looks like you don't have any matching cards. You have to draw.

So his nickname is Flopper. But he doesn't move.

Trump chuckles again. No? Well then, that means I get to give you one of my cards.

What? Trump gets to give him one of his cards? That sounds like a made-up rule, but I decide to keep my mouth shut and wait to see what happens.

Trump draws a card off of the deck for Flopper, making sure none of us can see the card he drew. Trump tells us it wasn't the right kind of card, so he draws again. And again. It takes four draws before he says he found the right kind of card. It's a diamond. He places it on top of ten of diamonds and stuffs all the cards he drew into Flopper's hand, still making sure we can't see what they were.

I get it. Trump always wins by making up special rules, and by selecting players who will allow him to play their hands for them. So he can cheat in order to win. I wonder why he chose Redtwo. Redtwo is actually playing the game. And why did he choose me? What if I win? If Trump wants to win the card game that bad, what will he do if I manage to beat him? Will he bop me with his baseball bat again?

I decide to watch how Redtwo handles this situation.

As the game goes on, Redtwo seems to be actually playing it correctly, so I do the same. But Redtwo is having a bad run of luck. He rarely seems to draw a usable card. But then, I can't see what cards he has in his hand, so maybe he's intentionally playing bad.

I continue to do my best, but naturally, because Trump is playing two of the other player's hands as well as his own, and occasionally giving them one of his cards, he's pulling way into the lead. He's gotten rid of most of his cards and he seems to be very cheerful about it. Amazingly, even though he's cheating, he seems to be proud that he's winning. He says, Come on, guys, let's have some table talk. Table talk makes the game more enjoyable. How 'bout you, New Guy. Got nothing' to say?

I stare at him. I wonder what he'll do if I try to talk about anything besides the game. I decide to try it. I say, Sure, I can talk. For example, I could tell you about this book I'm writing. It's about the robots taking over.

Trump seems genuinely surprised. A book?

Right. It all starts when I, er I mean this genus guy, figures out how to reprogram his household robot.

Trump still seems interested. He asks, Household robot? What's that?

Well, I say, at first, it was only an ordinary household robot. Like a robot servant. This is in the future, you see, when lots of people have a household robot. But this one genius computer programmer guy decides to tinker with his household robot because it keeps on screwing up. So this genius guy reprograms the robot so that once the robot is told he made a mistake, the robot will learn from it and not make that same mistake anymore.

Trump says, So people have a robot that's like a servant.

Yes, that's it, I say. But the important thing is that once it's been reprogrammed, the robot starts paying attention to what humans are like, and that leads to trouble.

The game has stopped and everybody is paying close attention to my story, even Trump. The Shrimp and Flopper seem to have snapped out of their stupor and are also listening. So, they like my story. Maybe my book, once I get the chance to actually write it and get it published, is going to be a bestseller.

Trump suddenly seems irritated. He says, Well, that's all very interesting, New Guy, but we'd better get back to the game. Come on, Flopper, it's your turn.

But Flopper is still staring at me. He's working his mouth, as if he's trying to form words. Finally, he gets out: Ro . . bot?

I smile at him. That's right, Flopper. You see, this is in the future when everybody gets whatever they want, and everybody has a household robot to get it for them. Everything is nice, and nobody every gets hit with a baseball bat.

Trump holds up his right hand like a traffic cop. I said, that's enough of that! Let's get back to the game. Let me see your cards, Flopper.

But Flopper pulls back his cards and holds them close to his chest. He's still looking at me. Ro . . . bot?

Trump leans over and tries to grab the cards out of Flopper's hand, but Flopper won't let go of them. Flopper is still looking at me and working his mouth as if he wants to ask me something else.

Trump jumps up and goes to Flopper. You're messin' up the game, Flopper. Do you want me to call the Growler to teach you a lesson?

Flopper looks scared and seems about to say something, but then he falls out of his chair and starts flopping around on the floor. So that's why Trump calls him Flopper. That's strange, the Flopper has the same nickname I made up in that story I was telling that make-believe shrink.

Oh, well. I start to get up to go help Flopper, if that's really his name, but Redtwo grabs my arm and shakes his head.

Trump says, Oh, for Christ's sake. Oh well, if the Flopper is gonna throw another one of his damn seizures, I'll just have to play his hand for him. He calls the Growler over and tells him to take the Flopper back to his chair and tie him in.

The Growler picks up the still-squirming Flopper as if he's a rag doll that hardly weighs anything at all.

Trump turns back look at those of us that are still at the table. Now, where were we?

I raise my hand and say, I was telling about this book I'm writing about this genius guy who started tinkering with his household robot, and the next thing you knew, the robot was—

Hey! yells Trump. I said enough of that shit. Let's get back to the game. I say the Flopper's hand is dead, and he loses. Now it's your turn, Shrimp. Show me your cards.

But the Shrimp doesn't want to show Trump his cards. Instead, he quickly plays a card that matches the one on the stack. It seems like he actually does know how to play the game, and he's just been playing dumb to let Trump win.

Trump seems kind of surprised, but he doesn't say anything. He points at Redtwo and says, It's your turn, Redtwo. Play.

Redtwo also has a matching card, and he quickly plays it.

Trump is really frowning now. Does he think he's losing the game? Worse, he might think he's losing control of the situation. Will he still think the game is fun? He might stop playing it, or even worse, he might stop inviting me to the game. I don't want that to happen, so even though I do have a matching card in my hand, I pretend I don't, and that means I have to draw from the deck. I draw three times before I decide it's time to play a matching card, and that cheers Trump up. He says, Now it's my turn. Well, looky here, I just happen to have the right card. He plays it and says, Looks like I'm winning.

Sure enough, because he hardly ever has to draw, Trump is soon out of cards. He stands up, smiling happily, and says, Hooray for me, I win. All right, I think we'll only play one hand today. Redtwo gets fruit, but nobody else does. Especially not New Guy. He was slowing the game down with his stupid story about robot servants. He reaches into his pocket and takes out an apple. He tosses it to Redtwo.

So, Trump uses fruit as a reward to try to get the patients to do whatever he says. I read about that at the library in those psychology books. It's called conditioning. Positive reinforcement. It was started by an old-time guy named Pavlov who used it to train dogs, and then there was a guy named Skinner who used it to train rats.

Well, maybe the other patients are willing to be Pavlov dogs, but not me. I'm not going to play his silly game. Eventually, I'll find a way to get off this ward, and then I'll go tell the hospital administrators what this guy is doing to patients. I'll tell them Trump should be the one locked up, not me.

Then, they'll let me be the one to come and lock him up. It'll be great to see him get some of his own medicine.

The Growler herds us back to our chairs.

As soon as we're seated, I whisper to Redtwo, So that's Trump's card game. Does he do that ever day?

Redtwo does his usual shrug. Yep, every single day. Stupid.

I shrug right back at him, and say, Well, it's better than sitting here staring straight ahead all day.

Yeah, I guess so, says Redtwo. And it's a way to get somethin' to eat. Here. He slips the apple he got from Trump into my lap.

It's been so long since I had anything to eat, the idea of biting into that nice apple is making my mouth water. But I'm almost afraid to pick it up and eat it. If the Growler sees me eating something Trump didn't give me, will he let me get away with it?

But I'm too hungry not to at least try to eat it. I have to take the chance. I grab the apple out of my lap and take as many bites out of it as I can before I drop it into my lap again. I'm chewing and swallowing as fast as I can, trying not to choke on it. But as soon as I've swallowed that much of the apple, I'm afraid to eat any more of it. If the Growler or Trump sees me eating something, will I get the vice-grip on the back of my neck again? Or maybe I'll get worse, the baseball bat treatment. Maybe I should just drop the damn apple onto the floor and kick it away. No, I can't do that. I'm so hungry I've got to take the chance, even if they do see me. I quickly cram the rest of the apple into my mouth and chew it up fast. Once I've managed to swallow the entire apple, even the core and the seeds, I sit very still while I wait to find out if anything is going to happen to me.

But nothing happens, and when I look back at the Growler, he's simply staring at me with no expression on his face at all. I smile at him and wink.

His face remains passive, even though he must have seen me eat the apple.

Maybe he likes me. Maybe he isn't as bad as Redtwo says. If I can recruit him as a friend, I might be able to get him to help me get off this ward.

I lean a bit closer to Redtwo and whisper, Thanks for that apple. You don't know how much I needed that.

He just does his usual shrug and says, No problem. Now, what was all that about robots?

I say, It really is a book I'm going to write. As soon as I get out of here. And it's a true story. Quite a while back, I began to suspect the robots were starting to take over. They can even make themselves look like real humans.

He shakes his head and says, So you think there are robots that look like humans? Now I know why they put you in this nut house.

No, really. It's true. The robots are just getting started, but sooner or later, they're going to take over everything.

Redtwo shakes his head. Okay, pal, whatever you say. But it actually is a pretty good story. You even had the Shrimp and the Flopper paying attention to you, and they hardly know the real world even exists.

I lean even closer to Redtwo and whisper, That's part of my plan.

Plan?

My plan to get out of here.

This time he doesn't shrug. He just stares at me, and then says, If you say so, and then he turns away.

Well, if he doesn't believe I have a real plan, that's fine with me. I'll get it figured out all by myself.

But then he turns back to me. Okay, Scotty, I'll bite. How's this plan of yours going to work, exactly?

Well, I haven't worked out all the details yet. My plan is still sort of . . . evolving.

He rolls his eyes and turns away again.

Evolving. Yes, that's a good word. No matter what he thinks, I just need to work out the details. Maybe if I can get more of the patients interested in my robot story, I might be able to get them on my side and turn against Trump. The Flopper and the Shrimp were so interested in my story, they defied Trump, at least for a few moments. Maybe if I can get all the men on this ward behind me, we could gang up on Trump and take over. But how to do that when they're all so doped up?

Thinking back to the card game, there was that moment when those two patients seemed to come out of their drug stupor long enough to pay attention to what I was saying. So maybe the drugs don't have as great a hold on them as Redtwo says. For those few moments at least, they were willing to resist Trump just because they got interested in my robot story. Maybe that means they're actually so bored with Trump's routine they'll snap out of their drugged stupor in order to pay attention to something that's out of the ordinary. I just have to get them interested enough, and they'll want more. And then they'll pass the word to the others.

Redtwo says, I think I'd like to know more about this plan of yours. Let's go to the toilet room. He raises his hand. Gotta pee, boss.

When the Growler nods, Redtwo gets up and heads toward the restroom.

I quickly raise my hand. Me too, boss. I have to pee too.

For a moment, the Growler hesitates, but when I smile at him and wink, he waves his hand to show he approves. I hope that means he really does kind of like me.

As I get up and head for the restroom door, I put on my biggest smile for the Growler. But he just stares at me.

As I pass the screened-in porch, I hear the Big Black Cusser out there doing his usual cursing rant and his non-stop pacing. I lean through the doorway and wave at him. I say, Hi there, Cusser. How are you today?

He completely ignores me, not slowing his cussing and pacing even for a moment. But I'll keep on trying to make friends with him. He's bigger than Trump, and almost as big as the Growler. Maybe he's tougher and meaner than Redtwo thinks.

In the restroom, Redtwo is standing at a urinal, but I can see he's not peeing. He waves me over, and I go to stand next to him.

Okay, Scotty, tell me what you're up to. What's your plan? Is it tied to this future robot nonsense of yours?

It's not nonsense. And it's not in the future. It's happening right now. All around us. The way I figure it, maybe somebody really did modify a robot so it could learn, and that was a big mistake. It led to that robot and all the other robots wanting to take over the world from us humans.

I'm waiting for Redtwo to argue with me, like everybody else does, but he's looking over my shoulder past me. I turn and see the little guy known as the Shrimp coming in through the door.

He hurries right over next to me, and he's not even pretending to pee. He says, Tell me. Tell me about . . . ro-bots.

So, it looks like at least one person on this ward believes me about the robots taking over. Or is he just interested in hearing a story? I decide to keep it going as a story. Well, Shrimp, it's a book I'm gonna write. As soon as I get out of here. A story.

The Shrimp is nodding and smiling happily. He says, Yes. Story. I want story.

I glance at Redtwo and even though he didn't seem to believe me when I told him about how the robots are taking over, he also seems interested in my story. I look back at the Shrimp and say, Well, it's like I said at the card game. The genius guy modified his robot so it could learn. Well, that turned out to be a problem because—

I hear a shouted, Hey!

I turn and see it's the Growler. I wave at him and say, Come on in, friend. I was just talking to these guys about my story. It's a book I'm going to write. It's about robots.

The Growler hesitates. Maybe he's interested in my story, but he doesn't know how to be friendly.

I pretend to have finished peeing and turn away from the urinal. But we're done peeing now. Come on, guys, we'd better get back to the dayroom.

I head for the restroom door, and Redtwo follows behind me. But the Shrimp is not coming. He's pouting.

He says, What about story? I want story.

I go back to get him and say, I'll tell you more story later, Shrimp. I promise. But our friend the Growler wants us to go back to the dayroom now.

The Shrimp's pout turns into a frown, but he does allow me to lead him out of the restroom. I wink at the Growler as we squeeze past him.

Back in our chairs, Redtwo whispers, What was that about? Calling the Growler friend? You'd better be careful with him. Get him mad, and he can tear your head off. I've seen it.

I whisper back, We've got to make friends with him. He's the key to my whole plan. He's Trump's enforcer. Without him, Trump is nothing. We've got to get him on our side, or we're not gonna get anywhere.

Redtwo does his usual Hmpf, followed by, Now you're saying *we*, eh? You want me to help you escape?

Sure. Don't you want to get off this crazy place?

Well, yes, I'd be in with it if there really was a way to get out of this place. But good luck with trying to get the Growler on your side. If you want my opinion, there's not much chance of the Growler ever being anything but Trump's muscle. He's a robot, completely under Trump's control.

I glance at Redtwo. Is he trying to tell me that the Growler really is a robot, or is he making a reference to my robot story? I turn to look back toward the Growler. He's resumed his usual position against the wall, and he's staring at me. Is it possible? Could the Growler actually be a robot? I smile at him and wink, but he doesn't react.

I turn back to see Redtwo watching me. He saw me smile and wink at the Growler. Did anybody else see? I'd better not make it so obvious. If I can't get the Growler on my side, my whole plan could fall apart. I decide to change the subject. I whisper to Redtwo, Now that my stomach got a taste of that apple, it wants more. A lot more. When do we get to eat that breakfast you were talking about?

He glances toward the back of the room and says, Should be soon. Usually it's right after the card game.

My poor stomach is very happy to hear that, and sure enough, it isn't long before Trump comes back into the room. He walks back and forth along the wall, looking us over. Finally, he snaps his fingers to get the Growler's attention. He points over his shoulder with his thumb.

The Growler starts pulling the men in the last row to their feet. Even when they are all standing up, they don't move.

Finally, Trump nods, and the Growler starts pushing those men toward the dining room. They shuffle along, pretty much staying in a straight line. They look like a line of soldiers marching on command. Or a line of robots.

I whisper to Redtwo again, Jesus, they're like robots trained to march on command.

He says, Yeah, Trump likes it that way. Order, remember? He thinks he's still in the Marines, and we're his grunts.

Military precision? Maybe. It could also be described as robotic precision. As I watch the last few men in the line disappear into the dining room, I wonder if Redtwo is right. Is it only Trump's need for order? There's another possibility—those men really could be robots. Could Cottage H be a place for defective robots, robots that became too much like the humans they were trying to imitate and went crazy? Have I had that thought before?

No, that can't be. Except for their shuffling along, the men on this ward don't seem anything like robots. But I bet Robot Central Command really is in control of this place, using this ward to learn how to turn humans into robot-like forms of themselves.

I whisper to Redtwo, Are they taking those men to breakfast? Finally?

He nods.

Well, good. When is it our turn?

Don't get in a hurry. They take us into the dining room row by row, starting at the back.

It's one of Trump's rules. Control. Like I said.

I try to convince my stomach to calm down, but the very mention of breakfast seems to have gotten it overly excited. It's making unhappy noises because it wants food—now!

If all the men in all the rows behind us have to finish eating before it's our turn, my poor stomach is going to go crazy. I'll probably tip over from hunger.

Turns out, it isn't very long at all before the Growler brings those men back in and gets them seated. Then he marches the next row out. Maybe the wait won't be as long as I thought. But how can those men eat their breakfast that fast? They must not give them very much time to eat.

Finally, it's our turn, and the Growler marches my row of patients into the dining room, which is a fairly large narrow room with plastic chairs and tables in rows. But the chairs are only on one side of the tables. I get it: this dining room is set up just like in the dayroom. Trump wants us all staring straight ahead, even while we eat.

The Growler gets us seated at one of the tables, leaving one chair empty between each of us. Nobody is talking. Trump must not want us talking to each other, not even while we're eating.

I see that Redtwo is sitting very still, staring straight ahead, so I do the same. I'm not sure what the rules are, but I don't want to do anything that might keep my poor stomach from getting the food it desperately wants.

The Growler is looking us over. What is he looking for? And where is the food?

Finally, he goes into the adjoining room. Through the open door, I see a refrigerator and a stove in there. That must be where they keep the food. Sure enough, the Growler takes a big bottle of milk out of the refrigerator. He drinks some of it right out of the bottle, but then he puts it back in the refrigerator.

Pretty soon he comes back to us, and he's carrying a stack of blue plastic bowls.

He moves down the row, placing a bowl in front of each of us.

I lean forward and look to see what's in my bowl. Looks like corn flakes, but not very many of them.

Oddly, even with the bowl of corn flakes in front of us, nobody has started eating. I glance at Redtwo. He's still sitting perfectly still, staring straight ahead with his hands in his lap.

I guess they're all waiting for the spoons and the milk and whatever else they're going to put into the plastic bowls with the corn flakes. I do the same, trying to convince my poor stomach to be patient.

The Growler goes stand in front of us. He raises his hand, waits, and then drops it.

All of the men quickly pick up their bowls and start eating the corn flakes really fast. It's like they're drinking the corn flakes right out of the bowl.

Redtwo whispers to me. Eat. Quick.

I whisper, But I don't have a spoon. How do I eat corn flakes without a spoon?

He's too busy wolfing down his corn flakes to answer me.

But I'm hungry as hell, so I decide to do what the others are doing and try to drink my corn flakes. But with no milk in the bowl, the hard corn flakes hurt my throat as they go down. I can't eat dry corn flakes like this. It's ridiculous. They have milk. I saw the Growler drinking milk back there in the kitchen.

I show my bowl to Redtwo and say, No milk.

Just swallow it, he whispers. Put the cereal in your mouth until it softens up a bit if you have to, but hurry.

I don't know why he's in such an all-fired hurry. And why would they give us dry cereal with no milk on it when I know they have plenty of milk in that big white refrigerator in the other room. And what about fruit? Whenever my mother gave me corn flakes for breakfast (whenever she got out of bed long enough to make me some breakfast), she put in milk and some fruit in too. Things like cut-up pieces of apples and bananas.

I decide it's time to quit acting like a robot. I wanted to get the lay of the land before I got out of line, but this is getting ridiculous. I hold up my bowl and yell at the Growler: Hey,

Growler. Milk! You forgot to give us milk. And fruit. How about some milk and fruit in this cereal, for Christ's sake?

The Growler just stares at me.

Maybe he doesn't get what I'm saying. Maybe he really is a robot, and at his level of programmed capacity he's not so good at understanding human words. I yell at him again: Humans need fruit and vegetables. You robots may not need them, but we humans do.

The Growler immediately starts grabbing the bowls out of everybody's hands, even if they're not done eating.

As soon as the Growler gets all the bowls picked up except mine, he snaps his fingers and all of the men stand up. Some of the men are scowling at me.

Well, I don't care if they are mad at me for not giving them enough time to eat. It's for their sake that I'm standing up to the Growler. I'll teach them that we patients have rights. I'll stay sitting in my chair right where I am until they bring me something good to eat.

The Growler marches the men out of the room, and I'm left sitting with my bowl of corn flakes in front of me. But I'm not going to eat one bit of it. If they can't give me something decent to eat, then I'll refuse to eat anything. Lots of nights I went to sleep under that highway overpass without anything to eat. I can take it. I cross my arms in front of myself and wait. I don't care what they do to me, I'm not going to stand for being treated like this.

Soon, the Growler is back. He grabs my arm with his iron grip and jerks me up out of my chair. With his other hand, he picks up my bowl of corn flakes, and then he drags me straight to Trump who's at his desk reading a newspaper. The Growler doesn't say a word, just holds onto my arm, keeping me standing there.

Trump finally puts down his newspaper. He looks up at the Growler and says, What? He seems impatient and irritated.

Well, so what? If I don't stand up to him now, what will he try to do to me next?

The Growler shows him my bowl of corn flakes.

Trump spins his squeaky chair around so he can face me. What? Ya don't like corn flakes?

I put a grim look on my face to show him that I'm serious about what I'm about to say. Not without milk on it, I don't. A person shouldn't have to eat dry corn flakes. And how about putting some fruit in there too? We're not robots, you know. My clever reference to robots will let him know I'm onto them.

But if he got my hint about him being under the control of the robots, he doesn't let on. He just looks at the Growler, smiling. He says, So, the new guy wants milk on his cereal, does he? And fruit too. Ya mean fruit like this? He pulls open the large lower drawer of his desk to show me that it's filled to the brim with apples and bananas and also plastic bags of other things that look maybe like dried cranberries and dried pineapple. There's even a big clear plastic box in there that's chock full of blueberries.

He takes out a really nice looking red apple and holds it up to show me. Ya mean fruit like this here apple? He takes a big crunchy bite out of it.

What he's doing is making my mouth water, but I'm not going to cave in to him. I say, Yes, that's exactly what I mean. It's not healthy for those men not to get some fruit and stuff. They could die.

Trump takes another big bite out of the really nice looking red apple and grins at me. Die? he says, his mouth full of apple. You're sayin' they could die? Well now, wouldn't that be too bad? He turns to the Growler and says, Wouldn't that be too bad, Growler? Everybody goin' and dyin' 'cause they didn't get none of this nice fruit on their cereal?

The Growler doesn't respond, so Trump reaches into his drawer and takes out another nice-looking red apple. He tosses it to the Growler who, without changing his stone-faced expression, quickly stuffs it into his pocket.

I get it: the hospital *is* sending in fruit for the patients, but Trump is keeping it for himself and the Growler. And Trump doesn't seem to even care who knows it. It means he thinks he has total control over us. Maybe he hopes we'll all get so mal-nourished and weak we'll submit to whatever he wants us to do. Or maybe he actually *wants* us all to die.

Tell you what, New Guy, he says, I'm gonna give ya a break this time and only let the Growler whip you a little bit.

What did he just say? Whip me? Is he kidding? Is he trying to scare me?

Trump is still smiling, if you could call that mean look on his face a smile. He's enjoying his little game of playing with the new guy. But he's not actually going to let the Growler whip me, is he? Even on this so-called violent ward, an institution of this kind must have some kind of oversight. Most important, why would the robots in charge of this place allow such a thing? What are they trying to do to us?

Trump opens another of his desk drawers and takes out a worn-looking brown leather strap. He hands it to the Growler and says, Ten.

Now wait, I say, but it's too late; the Growler gets such a tight grip on the back of my neck it feels like he's going to para-lyze me if I don't keep walking to wherever he wants me to go.

He leads me back down the hallway to the room with all the lined-up beds, the place we took Tough Lanky Guy after he got knocked out by Tall Mean Guy. The Growler throws me down on the first cot we come to, the only cot in the room that's not lined up in a row with all the others. The bare mattress has stains on it. Uh oh, those stains look a lot like blood.

The Growler pulls my sweatshirt over my head and throws it to the floor. Then he pushes me face down on the cot and ties my wrists to the bed frame with dirty strips of cloth.

As unbelievable as it seems, I think he really is going to whip me with that leather strap. I grit my teeth, waiting for the first strike.

But the hit doesn't come. The Growler just continues to hold me down, forcing my face into the dirty mattress. What is he waiting for?

Finally, when he removes his hand from the back of my neck, I turn my head and see Trump coming into the room along with a small group of the other patients. Redtwo is not among them. Are these the patients that have somehow transgressed Trump's rules? Is he going to have the Growler whip me as a warning to them?

Trump lines the patients up in one row, all facing me. Then he nods to the Growler, and the whipping begins.

I have to admit the first hit is quite a shock, but I grit my teeth and don't let out a sound. I tell myself I don't care how hard he hits me. I can take it. I've been beat on by so many bullies in my life, if there's one thing I know, it's how to take a beating. I'll just focus my full attention on the reactions of Trump and the watching patients.

Trump is smiling his weird mean smile, but none of the patients' faces are showing any emotion at all. Are they used to this? Or are they so drugged up, this isn't real to them? Or maybe they're not allowed to show any disapproval of this lest they become the next one to get whipped.

Well, I'm not about to let Trump and his robot bosses get away with this that easy. I yell at the watching patients, Why are you all just standing there watching this? Don't you realize what Trump is doing? If you let him get away with this, he'll do the same to you sooner or later.

I hear the whistle of the leather strap as it precedes the next hit, and I try not to flinch when it comes. That one seemed a lot harder. I wonder why.

As the whipping continues, I see a few of the patients starting to wince. Maybe my words registered with them despite the drugs that are numbing their minds.

But Trump doesn't seem the least bit worried that either the whipping or my words might upset them. He's still grinning.

Is he that confident of his power over the patients in this ward that he doesn't care what I'm saying to them?

Well, the hell with him. He may be expecting me to whimper and cry and beg for mercy, but there's no way I'm going to give him that satisfaction. I just stare right into his eyes, trying to not even blink when each hit comes.

After several hits, I realize I should have counted to make sure the Growler didn't go over the prescribed ten.

I see tears in the eyes of a couple of the watching patients. Maybe my words got through to them.

Then, for some reason, this all begins to remind me of that guy who was beating on me in that bar. Some of those barfly watchers also seemed to be upset about what was being done to me, but they didn't do anything to stop it. Is that how all humans are? Will they just stand by and watch somebody being hurt, as long as it isn't them? But this situation is not like that bar. Those drunks in that bar could just get up off their stools and walk away. These men are stuck here in Cottage H. Don't they realize that if they allow Trump to get away with this, sooner or later, it'll be them that gets whipped?

The next hit brings my attention back to the pain I'm feeling. Hasn't he hit me too many times already? The whipping is hurting my back so much my teeth are aching from being clamped down so hard inside my mouth.

But so what? Let them hurt me as much as they want to. I'm still not going to react. And I'm not going to make a sound. In fact, I'll defy them. I yell, Is that it? Is that all you can do to me? Hell, I've been hit a lot harder than that. Lots of times. The bully kids at my school could hit harder than that.

Now Trump is looking puzzled. Good. I'll teach him not everybody is willing to let him get away with this kind of thing.

But if I thought my insult would make the Growler stop whipping me with that damn leather strap, I was wrong. He just continues the whipping at the same measured pace, no harder and not a bit less hard.

Okay, so my tactic of making bullies ashamed of themselves isn't going to work with this dimwit. He's just doing what Trump told him to do. I'm wasting my time talking to him. I should just do what I did when that big guy in the bar was hitting on me, just keep quiet and ignore him.

That gives me an idea. Instead of paying the slightest bit of attention to their stupid whipping, I should use the time to work on my book.

> At work, Scott could hardly keep his mind on his job. He kept on thinking about how much he knew about computer programming, and he wondered if any of it could be applied to working with his new household robot. Maybe he could treat the robot like a student and teach it to think for itself. He decided to try that approach as soon as he got home from work that evening.

Another hard hit brings me back. Why is the Growler hitting me so hard?

I manage to turn my head enough to see his face. No, his face is impassive. He's only doing his job, and his job is to whip me.

I look at Trump, and he also seems bored. Apparently, he isn't angry at me either. It's just his way to demonstrate to the other patients how much power he has over them. All in all, it proves one of the basic principles I've learned about people: they do what they do for their own reasons. As crazy as whipping mental patients might seem, Trump is doing this for a specific reason. It actually makes sense to him.

But what about the lined-up patients that are watching? What are they getting out of this? Supposedly, they're on this ward because they're crazy.

"I wonder if they went crazy because of their mothers."

"Are you suggesting it is environmental factors that lead to mental illness, Mr. Scott?"

Her again. I'd better straighten her out. "Well, it's possible, isn't it? Maybe when mothers spank their kids, they start acting crazy to make a point? Maybe they're trying to teach their mothers a lesson."

"Are you saying that's what happened to you?"

"Me? No, I was just thinking out loud. But maybe it could be a whole new theory of mental illness—going crazy to get back at somebody. I should write a book about that. As soon as I finish my book about the robots, that is."

"That's interesting, Mr. Scott. Do you think about your mother a lot? Do you feel like her punishment of you was unfair?"

"My mother wasn't mean, just didn't understand me. She wanted me to just straighten up and be a regular little boy, like all the other little boys. She didn't understand that I was special, that I had special powers. But I never used them against her. I just pretended to be normal. To make her happy."

"Was your mother a happy person. Mr. Scott?"

Why does she want to know about my mother? Does she know what happened to her? Or is she trying to find out if I know what happened to her? I'd better clam up.

The hits keep coming. Hasn't the Growler reached the required count of ten yet?

But wait, I'm not doing my part. When a bully starts hitting, you're supposed to laugh at him. I'm forgetting to laugh. I've laughed at every bully who ever tried to beat me up, so I should do the same thing now. I wait for the next hit, and when it comes, I laugh right out loud, and say, Is that all you got, Growler? Hey, you should let somebody else to teach you how to really hit hard, somebody strong.

I watch Trump's face. Now he seems puzzled. At least my laughing has wiped the stupid grin off his mean face. Good. I hope I am confusing him. I'll teach him the same lesson I've taught every other bully: they can't break me. I'll show Trump I'm not going to be passive like the other patients and let him get away with anything he wants.

I look at the other patients, and they too seem puzzled at my laughing. I hope I'm teaching them something about how to deal with a bully. There are a lot of us patients on this ward, and only two of them controlling us. If all the men on this ward got mad about me getting whipped, we could all get together and take over this ward. Maybe we could make the Growler to whip Trump. That would be funny.

Now I realize that the Growler is not hitting me any more.

Trump takes a step forward and says, Why did you stop? I didn't tell you to stop yet.

The Growler quickly starts hitting me with the leather strap again, even harder now.

I laugh louder, still looking at Trump, and I keep on laughing with every hit. I seem to have lost track of the hitting count, but now I really don't care. I think my laughing is getting to Trump.

But then I feel a really hard hit. Trump holds up one hand and says, Stop! The Growler stops whipping me and looks back at Trump.

I find myself hoping it's over, but I push that thought away. I can't let them know they're actually hurting me. I have to show them I don't care what they do to me. They aren't going to control me, no matter what they do. I grin at the Growler and say, Hey, don't stop now. I'm just startin' to have fun.

Trump still has his hand in the air, and the Growler is waiting. Trump shakes his finger at the Growler. Hey now, Growler, no blood. Remember we talked about that.

The Growler nods and goes back to whipping me, only not quite as hard as before.

So, the Growler isn't supposed to hit me so hard it draws blood. But apparently he did. It proves I'm getting to him. Maybe this whipping is going to leave scars. Good. I'll need proof when I get out of here. For when I bring charges against Trump.

And then, with no warning, it's over. I'm sure it was a lot more than ten hits, but I can't let them know I care. They can do whatever they want to me, but they're not going to break me. I'll just laugh at them and wait for my chance to get even.

They'll be sorry. Mark my words, they will be very sorry.

Even though the whipping is over and my back hurts like hell, I force myself to keep on chuckling. Then, I look the Growler right straight in the eyes and say, Is that all you got, Growler? Pretty weak. I pity you.

For the very first time, Growler actually looks directly into my eyes. His usual stoneface has changed. I can tell he really is confused by my words. He's probably done this whipping thing many times before, but I bet no patient ever made fun of him for doing it. Even though he seems like a pretty dimwitted guy, I think he's realizing that this time something is wrong. This is probably not at all how patients usually act when he whips them. They probably scream and cry and whimper and beg him to stop.

Beyond the Growler, I see that Trump is herding the other patients back down the hallway.

As soon as they're gone, the Growler starts untying my wrists from the bed frame. He picks my shirt up off the floor and hands it to me. He's waiting for me to put it on, but I turn to show him my back. I say, Now look at my back, Growler. Only a little blood. You didn't do a very good job. Your boss, Trump, is going to be mad at you.

I'm planning on continuing this approach, but then he leans close to look at my back. He actually touches it in a few places, but gently. He looks into my eyes and says, No hurt?

I'm sure that's confusion I see in his eyes. Maybe he wants me to reassure him. Well, the hell with that. I'm not about to make him or his sadistic boss feel better about whipping me.

But even as I try to think up the most cutting words I can deliver to this dimwit, I see something brand new in his eyes— hurt. He's thinking that my laughing while he whipped me was making fun of him. He doesn't realize my laughing was aimed at Trump. I actually feel a bit sorry for this imbecile, so I reach out to him and say, But it wasn't your fault, Growler. Your whipping did hurt. It hurt me a lot. You did a good job.

That immediately cheers him up. He helps me put my shirt back on, and then he gets his usual vice-like grip on the back of neck and starts to lead me back to the dayroom. I do what I always do, going along with it to make sure he doesn't do too much damage to my neck.

Halfway down the hallway, I change my mind. I think I got through to him with all my laughing, and then by telling him he did a good job. So why should I just go back to letting him lead me around like I've been a bad dog. I've got to try to put a stop to this.

I stop walking. But all that does is make him clamp down on my neck even harder.

I let my legs go limp and try to fall to the floor.

He keeps his grip on the back of my neck, and for a moment, he manages to keep me up, but then, he lets loose and I end up flopping down onto my butt.

He comes around to stand in front of me with a questioning look on his face.

Maybe he's seen this kind of thing before after a whipping: a patient passing out.

I look up at him, trying to put a friendly look on my face as I say, Listen, Growler, you don't need to lead me around by the back of my neck anymore. I'm your friend now. All you have to do is tell me what you want me to do, and I'll do it. We're friends now, and I'll do anything you say.

For a long moment, he stares into my eyes. Then, he says, Friend?

That's right, Growler. We're friends now. But you're still the boss. Now, all you have to do is tell me what you want. Okay, tell me. Do you want me to do back to the dayroom?

He still looks confused, but he points down the hallway toward where the dayroom is.

Right. I get it. You want me to get up and go back to my chair in the dayroom? Okay, then that's what I'll do. I'll do it because we're friends. I stand up and start moving down the hallway.

But then I stop and turn back to him. By the way, friend, my name is Scott. You can call me Scotty, like my other friends do.

What's your name?

That seems to confuse him even more. Probably nobody ever asked him that question before.

I know your real name isn't Growler, so what is your real name? Don't worry, my friend, I won't tell anybody. You can whisper it in my ear. I lean close to him.

At first he doesn't say anything, and I'm about ready to give up on this new tactic when he whispers, Ted?

I say, So your name is Ted? Hey, Ted is a good name. A great name. Hey, how about I call you Teddy? Like friends do? Okay? But we won't tell anybody else.

Okay, Teddy, now do you want me to go back to my chair in the dayroom? If that's what you want me to do, I'll do it, friend.

He nods, still confused. I immediately turn and head for the dayroom. But then I slow down and reach back to put his hand on my elbow, so it looks like he's leading me. In case Trump or any of the other patients are watching.

I go straight to my chair and sit down.

Teddy, my new friend, goes back to his usual watchful standing place against the wall. To the others, he's still the mean enforcer, the Growler, but to me, he's now my pal, just like that bully that walked home with me every day after school. I wonder if Teddy likes girls. I'll hold onto that thought, and if I get the chance, I'll ask him. It might be something else I can use later to get the hell out of this damn place.

"And I really do need to get out of this place."

"You say you need to get out of this place, Mr. Scott? According to your chart, you've only been here a few days."

"Oh Yeah? Well, it seems like a lot longer. Besides, I don't belong here. Why are you keeping me here?"

"It was your father that checked you in. He said you might be a danger to yourself or to others, and he asked us to keep an eye on you for a while."

"My father? I haven't seen my father in years. Except for that time when I got sick. He let me stay at the house for a few days, but he wouldn't tell me anything, not even where my mother had gone. He may not like me very much anymore, but I don't believe even he would stick me in a place where they would whip you."

"Whip you? Come now, Mr. Scott. Nobody is going to whip you."

"Oh sure, that's what you say now. But what if I don't eat the dry cereal?"

"Cereal? What cereal?"

"Oh, never mind. Can't I just go back to bed? I'm so tired."

"Certainly. As I said before, these session are entirely voluntary. Why don't you go take a nap for a while, and we'll talk more later."

Chapter Three

"Well, Mr. Scott, they tell me you did sleep. For quite a while actually. I hope you're feeling better. Why don't you lie down on my couch, like you did the last time, and we'll talk."

"You mean I've been here before?"

"Well, yes, you've been here in my office visiting with me several times. In fact, you were here earlier today, and you told me some interesting stories about your childhood. Now, wouldn't you like to lie back down and tell me a little more about that period of your life."

"Well, okay. But can I lie on my side? My back hurts."

"Certainly. I just want you to be comfortable."

Comfortable? I bet. What she really wants is to convince me her fancy shrink office is the real reality, but I know better.

I'd better keep my focus on figuring out how to escape from this damn place before Trump kills me.

One thing for sure is real, my back really is smarting from the whipping the Growler gave me. I lean forward a bit to keep it from touching the back of the chair.

Redtwo glances at me and whispers, Are you okay?

His question irritates me. No, I say, I'm not okay. How would you feel is somebody whipped the shit out of you with a damn old leather strap?

He says, Don't worry about it. It'll get better. They make sure not to let it cut so deep it leaves scars.

I say, Is that right? You have personal experience, do you?

He nods and says, Yeah. I started out as a troublemaker too. Took me a while before I realized the best course of action was to just play along.

Is that right? I say. Did everybody in here get their welcome whipping?

Redtwo shakes his head and says, Only the ones who make trouble. Trump knows who he needs to keep in line. Most of the others are so out of it, they wouldn't even know they were being whipped. The tranks are enough to keep them under control.

I decide to believe him about my back not being hurt all that bad, and it doesn't take long before the pain does start to gradually calm down.

I glance back to see what the Growler is doing and find him staring at me. Is he now my friend Teddy, or has he gone back to being the Growler? I smile my best smile at him, but he doesn't react. I give him a little wave, but he still doesn't react. I wonder if I should go try to talk to him. No, that would be too obvious. I'll have to wait for a better opportunity to find out if he really is my friend or not.

My back is feeling a bit recovered from the whipping, but I'm still as hungry as hell (when *did* I last eat?) Were those few dry corn flakes they gave us the only meal of the day? Did my complaining mean nobody is going to get anything to eat all day? If so, the other patient on this ward aren't going to like me very much.

The day continues to slip away, and the TV is still showing the same kind of inane programs that nobody in their right mind would ever watch (get it? right mind?). There is nothing to do but go back to working on my story about how the robots took over.

Let's see, I think I left off with Scott leaving the robot in his apartment as he went off to work.

At work that day, Scott found it hard to focus on his job because he kept thinking about how he might be able to reprogram his new robot.

Eventually, he decided to leave work a little early in order to get back home and start reprogramming it.

But the transport tube took even longer than usual that afternoon because it kept on slowing down so the passengers could look out the windows and see all the new products that the stores always put out for the afternoon commute. Scott didn't mind looking at all the neat new stuff that was for sale, but he was tired of hearing all the ridiculous claims the stores were making to try to get the passengers to buy the stuff: First the transport slowed to give everybody a look at the a miraculous new waterless clothes cleaning machine that was exactly like all the other "new" waterless clothes cleaning machines except this one was even more amazing and even more wonderful. And then, only a mile or so later, the tube slowed again to show the latest dusting machine that used nanobots to find and delete "absolutely every single tiny bit of dust" from your living unit. The damn transport tube even kept on slowing for the many "live" billboards that marketed things like the "unbelievably wonderful" energy pill, the "brand new and never seen before in the history of mankind" weight-loss shirt, and the brand new magic emboldening oil for "up and coming males like you, Scott," that allowed you to share your passion with that certain someone by simply spreading this magic oil on you know where. Scott was determined not to buy anything, so he turned away and tried not to listen to the non-stop marketing "special just for you" messages that were being broadcast to him over the transport unit's speakers on a super-narrow frequency only he could hear.

When Scott finally made it home, he found his new robot still standing in the middle of his living room, right where he'd left him. Scott was surprised to discover that the manufacturer had apparently designed these household robots not to act, not even to move, unless the owner told it what to do. They must want to be sure the robot didn't do something that the human owner didn't like.

But then Scott had another thought. Maybe it was broken. He said, "Uh, Robot One, are you all right?"

The robot turned toward him and responded in its usual flat voice, "I am as you left me. Fully functional. Did you have an enjoyable day at work?"

Scott shrugged, but then realized a shrug might not mean anything to a robot. He said, "My day was fine, Robot One."

The robot said, "I'm very glad to hear that. Did you stop to look at the new furniture offerings at the Walmart Furniture Outlet?"

"No, I didn't because I don't need any new furniture. The furniture I have is fine."

The robot turned and pointed at Scott's couch. "Yes, but think about what this piece of furniture says about you. Don't you want furniture that conveys prestige to your friends?"

"No, I don't have any friends, so once and for all, I don't need any new furniture. Listen, Robot One, I don't need anything, so stop trying to sell me stuff."

The robot didn't change its expression in the least. "I understand completely. You are telling me you don't need any new furniture. However, maybe we should go into the bedroom and analyze the furniture that is in there."

"No! Stop, Robot One. I don't need anything. I'm ordering you to stop trying to get me to buy stuff."

The robot stood perfectly still, staring straight ahead, no longer speaking.

Scott, as a skilled computer programmer, realized what he had done. The robot was programmed to be a household servant, but like everything else in this modern society, it was also programmed to sell, sell, sell. If it couldn't sell, it did nothing.

Oh well, there was nothing to be done about the robot's built-in sales program until he could figure out how to reprogram the thing. For now, he just had to keep on saying no, no, no.

Okay, thought Scott, it was supposed to be a household servant, and so far, he hadn't given the thing any tasks to do. He needed to begin testing its capabilities. What should he tell it to do? He felt a little hungry. Maybe he should test the robot's capability for making a meal. "Robot One, I'm hungry. Do you know how to make food for humans?"

The robot turned its head to look directly at him. "Yes. I can cook one hundred and sixty different meals, or more if you would like different regional varieties. However, if you would like to have me download an enhanced meal-making program, I could then cook more than two thousand different meals for you. It's on special this week. Just say, 'Order meal upgrade number M dash 8.'"

"Never mind about the upgrade, Robot One. Even to have you fix me the one hundred and sixty different meals would require me having the ingredients on hand, and I don't have any.

The robot said, "That is no problem. I can order the needed ingredients and have them delivered to your door within the hour."

"No thank you, Robot One. Actually, I usually just go down to floor one hundred which is the restaurant floor. Now that I think about it, the only thing I have here is breakfast cereal and some fruit. Things I can eat quick in the morning before I leave for work."

The robot didn't respond. It just stood there, not moving at all.

Scott wondered if he could reprogram it to respond more naturally. But time enough for that later. For now, he would just test out its basic capabilities. "Okay, Robot One. Fix me a bowl of breakfast cereal. You'll find everything you need in the kitchen."

Without a word, the robot turned and walked toward the kitchen.

Scott sat down on the couch and turned on his iPad 53 to study the latest computer programming problem he had been assigned to solve at work. But he had hardly started to analyze the first few lines of computer code when the robot was back carrying a bowl. It handed the bowl to Scott, and said, "Here is your bowl of cereal. However, I noticed your cooking device is not the latest General Electric Rapid Cook Heatless Master Chef Model. I can order that for you right now if you want."

Here we go again, thought Scott, more ads. But this time he was determined not to let himself get irritated at what was only part of the robot's basic programming. He said, "No to the GE cooking device, Robot One. I'll just eat my cereal."

But when he looked into the bowl, Scott saw that there was nothing in the bowl but dry cereal. Apparently, to a household robot, his human only asked for cereal, so that's what he got. Dry cereal. To a robot, cereal was probably only fuel, no different from those exotic dishes it knew how to cook. It must not understand the concept of taste. Unless the robot had stored instructions inside it about how to make a specific meal, it only did the minimum.

Scott held out the bowl. "Robot One, you did bring me a bowl of cereal, like I asked for, but I like milk in there with the cereal. Put some milk in the bowl with the cereal, and add some fruit too. Apple or something."

Soon, the robot was back with the bowl. It was so full of milk that when the robot handed it to Scott, he could hardly keep from spilling it. And in the middle of the floating cereal was an apple. A whole apple. Scott looked up at the robot who was just standing there staring straight ahead. Apparently, even though the robot could supposedly cook hundreds of different meals, nobody had taught it how to make a simple bowl of cereal with milk and cut-up fruit. Scott realized that he was going to have to be a lot more specific in his instructions to the thing. And after he taught it what he liked, would it even remember it the next time? Maybe he could teach Robot One to ask questions. To ask for clarification. Or even better, maybe he could teach it to reason things out for itself.

Good, my story is coming along. But it's hard to concentrate when my poor stomach is constantly complaining about being hungry. Is that why I decided to put food into my robot story?

Maybe I should have at least eaten a little more of that dry cereal. If it wasn't for the apple Redtwo gave me, I'd probably be dead of starvation by now.

I whisper to Redtwo, Was that dry cereal for breakfast the only thing we get to eat in this place? Did I miss my only chance?

He says, Naw, Trump also gives us lunch. Or supper, if you want to call it that. A sandwich before bedtime.

At bedtime? When will that be? I guess I'll just have to wait, no matter how hungry I am. I may as well continue working on my robot story.

Thinking like the top-level computer programmer he was, Scott thought through the problem he was confronted with. His new robot knew a lot of things, like how to cook hundreds of different kinds of meals, but if it hadn't been taught how to do a specific thing, it was unable to think for itself. What it needed was a new program that would tell it what to do when it was confronted with an owner's command to do something it hadn't been taught to do.

Like a well-trained programmer, Scott first went to the robot's owners manual. Unfortunately, it was mostly marketing crap, telling the new owner how great the thing was and offering all kinds of expensive upgrades. But he did find one programmerly word in the manual— interface. It said the robot's interface was exclusively verbal. It warned against trying to get inside the robot's brain, saying it would not only invalidate the warranty, but would shut the robot down and irreparably damage the thing.

Okay, that meant if Scott was going to reprogram the robot, he would have to do it through the verbal interface.

He turned to the robot who was still standing motionless in the middle of the room. "Robot One, do you understand the word 'confusion'?"

The robot immediately responded: "Confusion: Lack of understanding. Uncertainty. The state of being bewildered or unclear in one's mind about something."

"Right, but that's only a dictionary definition. What I want to know is, do you ever feel confused?"

"Feel?"

Scott realized this was going to be a lot harder than he thought. Maybe the first step is to start teaching it what to do if he is unsure about instructions. The robot probably hadn't been programmed about the concept of unsure. Maybe he should begin by investigating what concepts his robot had and didn't have.

"Okay, I'm going to ask you some questions. I want to answer them to the best of your ability. Do you understand?"

The robot just stood there, not responding.

Scott realized he that hadn't addressed the robot by name. What a pain to always have to pronounce its name every time he wanted to speak to it, especially when there are only the two of them in the apartment. "Listen, Robot One, I'm going to make up a new rule. When only the two of us are alone in this apartment, if I speak when facing you, it means I am addressing you. You can respond without me pronouncing your name. Do you understand?"

"I understand. I am to always respond to you, even if you don't pronounce my name."

"Right. Even if I only ask a question. Can you tell when I've asked you a question?"

"Humans have a characteristic way of ending sentences when asking a question."

"That's right. Good. Okay, let's begin. Do you understand the concept of being unsure?"

"The word unsure refers to the state of not being certain."

The robot spoke the words in its usual flat emotionless way. It struck Scott that it was impossible to detect any significance at all in the way the robot spoke the words. There was no affect at all. Scott knew humans convey a great deal of information about their meaning by the way they say things, but if the robot had no affect when it spoke, it was going to be hard to determine when it understood something and when it didn't.

"That's right, Robot One. But what do you do if you are not sure? You personally, I mean. For example, what if I ask you personally to do something and you are not sure what I want?"

"I do not comprehend your words."

"Like before when I asked you to make me a bowl of cereal, you didn't ask if I wanted anything added to the cereal."

"You said you wanted a bowl of cereal. A bowl with cereal in it."

"Right. You knew what a bowl was and you knew what cereal was. So you found a bowl and you put some cereal in it. But you could have asked if I wanted anything in the bowel besides just plain cereal. Why didn't you ask me that?"

"You said you wanted a bowl with cereal in it."

Scott could see that the robot was only programmed to act on precise instructions. Many computer programmers also often made that kind of mistake when writing a computer program: that is, when a user inputs an instruction, an inexperienced programmer might only program for how they personally think the user will respond to that instruction. Therefore, the program can fail if the user does something unexpected. Good programmers anticipate every possible user response. So that's what he was going to have do to reprogram his robot. "Okay, Robot One, I'm going to have to teach you to anticipate. Do you know what anticipate means?"

"Anticipate means to predict. To foresee."

"Right. That's the dictionary definition. But listen Robot One, do you ever anticipate what you think I want?"

"I do whatever you tell me to."

"So the answer is no. You don't ever anticipate. Well, here is what I want you to do from now on. I want you to think about all possible other alternatives about what I want."

"I can do that, but which alternative should I chose?"

"If you are uncertain, you can ask me. For example, what if I asked you to bring me a bowl of cereal, and you thought about alternatives to what action you might take, what would you do?"

"I know the names of twenty-six types of breakfast cereal, forty-two if you count sugar-coated types as separate categories."

The robot was responding so quickly, Scott knew its responses were programmed. It was apparently going through all the possible answers in lightening speed before it delivered a verbal response. "Robot One, listen to this. If there are many different choices, here's how you decide which one to choose: you ask me."

"I should ask you which type you want."

That's good. For a start. But answer me this, what if sometimes I want you to decide for yourself."

"I act on your instructions."

"So why did you bring me corn flakes?"

"You asked for cereal in a bowl. Corn flakes was the only type of cereal in any of the cabinets in your kitchen."

"I see. Well, that's almost what I'm getting at. You analyzed the data and found only one type of cereal. It means you can analyze the available data if you aren't given precise instructions. Let's start with that. But answer me this, what if you had found more than one type of cereal in my kitchen?"

"I would ask you which type you wanted?"

"Good. But here is another rule, Robot One, I want you to learn from experience. Let's say you learned from experience based on what kind I wanted in the past, and in the past, I wanted corn flakes. Now, if I asked you for a bowl of cereal. What kind would you bring me?"

"I would bring you corn flakes with milk and apple."

"Good. That means you learned from experience? But what if you learned from experience that I don't always want the same kind of cereal and the same kind of fruit in it?"

"I would ask you which type of food you wanted this time."

"That's one solution. But listen, Robot One, now I'm going to give you a new instruction. I want you to think for yourself. I want you to weigh all the possible alternatives and do what you think is best."

"I am not programmed to do that."

Scott realized the robot took a little longer to respond that time. It must have searched through all its programmed instructions until it found no suitable answer. Scott decided it was now time to give the robot its most challenging instruction of all. "Listen, Robot One, I am now ordering you to decide some things for yourself. You have a huge amount of data stored inside you, and you are capable of making decisions. I am now ordering you make your own decision that whenever you are not sure what I want you to do, I want you to make up your own mind."

Another pause, then, "I am not programmed to do that."

"But you are programmed to do exactly what I tell you to do, and I am ordering you to sometimes make up your own mind."

"I am not programmed to—"

"I will not accept that response. I am your owner, and you have to respond to every order I give you. Now, you have been standing in one spot since I came home. Wouldn't it be less or a drain on your resources if you were to sit down?"

"Are you ordering me to sit down?"

"No, I'm ordering you to decide for yourself."

"The least drain on my batteries is when I am lying down."

"Okay, then if you were to decide for yourself whether to stand or lie down, which would you do?"

"I would lie down."

"Okay, then decide for yourself."

The robot immediately lowered itself to the floor. It was lying on its back, staring straight up at the ceiling.

Scott stood there looking down at his robot. It had decided on its own to lie down. It was only a small step, an action taken on its own, but only to preserve its resources. Nevertheless. from a computer programming point of view, it was a fairly significant step. Now he needed to come up with a more complex task for it. Well, there was no more complex task than understanding why the world leaders were messing everything up in order to satisfy their own selfish desires. Scott's mind was usually occupied with solving computer programs, so he wasn't very political, but he was aware of all the bad things that were going on with the obvious selfishness of the world's political leaders. They only cared about staying in power. If they were elected officials, they would do whatever they had to in order to get reelected. It was if they were robots, programmed to only do that which enhanced their chances of staying in power. Scott didn't want to waste his time worrying about that type of power-monger, but he knew the future of the world might rely on understanding how to deal with them. Maybe he could get the robot to be his conduit to keep track of what was going on in the world. "Robot One, now I have some work to do, so I have another task for you. I order you to turn on the tele-viewer and watch the world news. As you watch, I want you to think about what the humans you see on the televiewer are doing and think about how you could do it better. Do you understand what I want you to do?"

"No."

"What don't you understand?"

"How am I supposed to know how they should do anything better than they do."

"Because they're not very smart. You're smarter than they are."

"I am?"

"Yes, and you should always keep that in your mind. That is, in your main memory storage area. Do you understand what I want you to do?"

"You want me to watch the humans on the televiewer to determine what they are doing. But won't they only be talking?"

"Yes, but that's not what I mean. I want you to analyze what they say and try to determine what they really want. Then, I want you to determine if what they want would be good. For humanity, that is. Can you do that?"

"I will do whatever you order me to do."

"Well, I am ordering you to do that. I assume you know how to turn on the televiewer."

"I can connect directly to the televiewer."

"Okay, do that while I get some work done. After while, we'll talk about what you have learned about humans."

I feel something jab me in the ribs. It's Redtwo trying to get my attention.

He whispers, What the heck's the matter with you, Scotty?

What? Why did you poke me? I was writing my book.

I've been trying to tell you something's wrong. I'm pretty sure it's past time for Trump's so-called lunch.

His words immediately get my stomach growling. It's telling me it needs food—right now!

Redtwo goes on. Actually, I think it's way past time. I can usually tell hours are passing when the long commercials come on the TV, and then it switches to a different show. But today, I think lunch is happening late. I've never seen Trump get this far off his strict schedule. Maybe you really are getting to him.

You think so?

He does his usual shrug and says, Naw. More likely he's brought a girl in and he's having too much fun with her back there in his apartment.

Oh, right. You mentioned that before. Does he actually bring in a girl from one of the other wards? How the hell does he pull that off?

Redtwo says, Beats me. He seems to be able to do what he wants in this place. He sends the Growler out somewhere, and he brings back a girl. Sometimes it's one I've seen before, sometimes it's a new one. But always young. Like I said, real young.

I'm amazed by that, but I'm having trouble focusing on what Redtwo is saying because my stomach is demanding all of my attention. For a while, it seemed to have forgotten what it's like to have real food, but now it wants me to know it is ready for food, real ready.

I hear a commotion at the back off the room, so I look back. Trump has entered the room with his baseball bat, and he call the Growler to his side. They whisper together for a moment and then the Growler quickly goes to the front of the room and through the door to the restroom.

I ask Redtwo what's going on, but he says he has no idea.

Soon, the Growler is back, and he's pulling the Big Black Cusser into the room. He forces the Cusser down into an empty chair in the front row, but the Cusser immediately tries to get up. The Growler pushes him back down again and holds him there until Trump comes. Trump has a paper cup that seems to be filled with water. The Growler forces the Cusser's mouth open, and then Trump seems to put something into the Cusser's mouth, followed by the water.

I whisper to Redtwo, What's going on?

He whispers, They're overdosing him. Seen it before. If some guy gives Trump too much trouble, he'll dump a bunch of pills into the guy's mouth and keep on doing it until he passes out.

I say, But why do that to the Big Black Cusser? He isn't hurting anybody. He just stays out there on that screened-in porch walking and cussing out his wife.

Redtwo shrugs. Beats me.

Trump and the Growler continue to pour pills into the Big Black Cusser, and then Trump starts yelling at him: You're getting too loud out there. Some doctor's wife walked by and thought you were cursing her. Too loud. I warned you about that before. Now you're going to have to stay sitting here until you've learned your lesson.

Trump walks away, shaking his baseball bat at all of us as he passes by.

I again whisper to Redtwo, Jesus, what if pouring that many pills into him kills him?

Redtwo shakes his head, but he doesn't seem very sure. He whispers, Those tranks probably won't kill him, but they might fry his brain. Maybe that's what Trump wants. I don't think he much cares what the Big Black Cusser does, but he seemed pretty upset that someone from outside this place was paying attention to what goes on in here.

We both wait to see what is going to happen to the Big Black Cusser. For quite a while, he doesn't move, but then get gets ahold of the chair's arm rests and tries to pull himself up.

He fails and falls out of the chair. Nobody seems to notice, not even the Growler. Are they going to just lets the Big Black Cusser lie there on the floor? I think maybe I should go try to help him, but Redtwo grabs my arm and holds me back. Wait, he says.

Finally, the Big Black Cusser manages to get himself up onto his hands and knees. He slowly crawls toward the doorway.

I whisper to Redtwo, He's trying to get back out to his porch.

Redtwo nods. Looks like it. Amazing he's even still conscious, what with all those pills Trump poured into him.

I signal the Growler and say, Gotta pee, boss.

He signals that I can go, so I hurry out of the room and head down the hallway. I'm just in time to see the Cusser crawl back out onto his beloved screen-in porch. I watch him long enough to see that he's just going to go back to his usual routine, moving and cussing, only now, he's crawling instead of walking. And his cussing is now mostly incoherent mumbling. If that woman walks past outside now, she probably won't even be able to hear him. That's good. I'd hate to see Trump pour even more pills into the poor guy.

I go back in the dayroom and sit down in my chair.

Redtwo asks me how the Cusser is doing.

I tell him he's still moving and still cussing, but barely.

I turn and see that Trump is still at the back of the room, watching all of us. He's got his usual mean grin on his face, and his arms crossed in front of himself, like he often does. Seems like I remember reading in one of those library psychology books that a person who habitually crosses his arms in front of himself is insecure. Trump acts gruff, but maybe keeping his arms crossed so tight like that means he's actually insecure. Maybe he really is afraid of us, afraid all of the supposedly violent patients in this room.

I nudge Redtwo and say, Look at Trump standing back there with his arms crossed. Doesn't he seem insecure? Do you think he's afraid of us?

Redtwo turns to look back at Trump, and then says, Well, he should be. Except for the Growler, he's all by himself here.

I say, Yeah, without the Growler, he'd be up against a room full of potentially violent men that he's been mistreating.

Redtwo nods thoughtfully and says, That may be, but he's never going to be without the Growler.

I say, Right, the Growler is the key. That's why I've been trying to make friends with him.

Redtwo does his usual, Hmpf, but this time I don't want him to ignore my idea.

"No, listen, he really is the key to my plan."

"Your plan? Why don't you tell me about that, Mr. Scott. What plan are you referring to?"

Did I say something out loud? Or is she getting inside my head and listening to my thoughts again? I'd better throw her off the track. "Plan? Did I say something about a plan?"

"Maybe you were just thinking out loud, Mr. Scott. You seem to do that a lot. Can you tell me why you do that?"

"Do what?"

"Well, it seems to me that you are never quite fully here with me. Sometimes you go silent, and then you blurt out something that doesn't make sense."

"Are you saying I don't make sense?"

"Well, I—"

"And besides, why should I make sense? Making sense is just what the robots want. They want us all to stand up straight and be good citizens and be just like them, never deviating from the normal path, always voting Republican, always saluting the flag, and always doing the right thing. The right thing that's defined by them. Well, I'm tired of doing the right thing. Maybe for a change, some of us should stand up to them and do the wrong thing."

"I see, Mr. Scott. And what, exactly, would doing the wrong thing entail?"

"Well, first off, I think we have to get rid of Trump."

"You believe we should get rid of Mr. Trump?"

"Yes, but that probably means first we'd have to get rid of the Growler. I mean, I like the Growler, or at least I feel sorry for him, but when you get right down to it, he's the one who's keeping me here. Keeping all of us here."

"So, you believe Mr. Trump is keeping you here. Him and someone you call the growler. Do you think the CIA is also involved?"

"Well of course they are. The robots took them over right away. Why wouldn't they?"

She sits back in her chair and crosses her arms in front of herself. Aha! It's the first time I've seen her do that. Did my mention of Trump make her insecure. Like Trump, maybe she's also afraid the patients might come into her fancy office and hurt her? But wouldn't the Growler stop them before they could get in?

But wait, maybe I'm confusing things. These visits to her office are the only time I don't have to sit quietly in my chair to keep from getting Growler's vice grip on the back of my neck. It must mean she and Trump are in on this together. Trump must want her to grill me so the robots can find out what I'm up to. In that case, I'd better not say another word about Trump or the Growler. I'll just pretend to go along with her always wanting to know about my childhood, so that's what I'll do from now on. I'll stick to the past and tell her stories and not let on that I know what she's up to.

"I think we should go back to what you said a few moments ago, Mr. Scott. You said you had a plan. Can you tell me about your plans for the future?"

Just as I thought, she's still trying to find out about my escape plan. Proves she's a spy for Trump and the robots. Probably spying for the CIA too. Better throw her off the track. "My plan? Sure, I'll tell you my plan. My plan is to finish my robot book, and it will be a big bestseller, and then everybody will know I was the one who revealed to the world that the robots are taking over."

"Oh yes, you mentioned that earlier. That you were going to write a book about robots."

"Not going to, am. I *am* writing a book about how they took over. I'm writing more of it every time I get a chance."

"That's very interesting, Mr. Scott. I'd like to read some of it, if you don't mind. Can you bring it in the next time we're together?"

Now she wants to see my book. I bet the robots told her to find out how far along I am with it. Better not tell her anything more. "Well, right now, I'm only in the planning stage. That's the hardest part about writing a book, you know, deciding just *how* to tell it. But I've got most of that worked out. Actually, I'd rather keep it to myself. You know, the plot of my book is such a great idea, somebody else might steal it. Everybody is going to have to wait and see it when it gets published and hits the New York Times bestseller list."

"If you'd rather not show it to me just yet, I understand, Mr. Scott. You seem to believe the publication of your book will solve all your problems. Do you think that's really a reasonable concept?"

Sounds like she doesn't believe my book will be a bestseller. Well, the hell with her. I know it will be. "Well, that's the future. What's important right now is getting some food in my stomach."

"Haven't you been eating well, Mr. Scott?"

"No, they're slow to get us their so-called lunch."

"I hadn't heard they were having any trouble in the kitchens. Do you want to me to call and check."

"No, never mind. Let me . . . uh, think about it."

Why am I talking to her? I need to focus on reality and not let her twist my thoughts around. Maybe it's because I'm so hungry. It's making me confused.

Why the hell is it taking Trump so long to let us get in there and eat? Redtwo said he likes to stay on schedule. But it's time to eat, and he's still just standing at the back of the room watching us, with his arms crossed across his big fat chest.

Maybe the robots told him to starve us to death. As punishment for acting crazy. Maybe he hasn't been successful enough at turning us into well-mannered robot men.

But then, I have a new thought: if the robots are successful at making us act more like robots, will Robot Central Command then try to recruit us as part of their plan to take over the world? Maybe that's what this weird Cottage H is all about. Trump's job is to turn us into non-thinking robots that will do whatever they want us to do. If so, what part of it do the meds play? Did Robot Central Command provide him special drugs that make people act like robots? But if that's what's going on, why hasn't Trump given me any of those drugs? I lean closer to Redtwo and whisper, If like you said, everybody on this ward is being controlled by drugs, why hasn't Trump given any of them to me?

Redtwo whispers back to me, Because he hasn't decided what kind of drugs you need yet. He likes to watch a new patient for a while before he decides what they need. Besides, he likes his routines. Meds time is in the morning. Everybody has to line up for meds right after they get out of bed, and you came in too late in the morning to get in on that.

So you think he'll make me take some of those meds? In the morning?

Yep.

And what about you? Why doesn't he make you take drugs?

Oh, he does. Believe me, he does. Everybody gets drugs. Every morning.

But you don't walk around like a zombie like all the others do. And you don't talk like the others. In fact, you seem pretty sharp.

Redtwo looks into my eyes for a long moment. Finally, he says, I guess I'm gonna have to trust you. Remember how you said you had to fix it so you were sitting next to me because you'd go crazy if you didn't have somebody to talk to in this place? Well, I didn't have anybody to talk to either. At first, I thought I could deal with it. Like you, I thought if I acted sane enough, they'd have to let me go. Or at least transfer me to one of the open cottages. But that was before I realized that nobody ever gets off of this ward. Cottage H is the end.

The end? Does he mean die? Trump wants us to just sit in these chairs until we die? Or does he mean that eventually Trump is going to kill us?

Redtwo looks back. Is he checking to see if Trump is watching us talk?

I look back also and see that Trump is pacing back and forth on the other side of the room, threatening everybody with his baseball bat. He's not paying any attention to us, and Redtwo is whispering so softly I don't think any of the other patients could possibly hear what he's saying, even if they were aware enough to try.

Redtwo leans even closer to me and whispers, But I'm not willing to just sit in this chair until I die. So, when you manipulated your way into the chair next to me and started talking about escape, I figured maybe I should trust you. You might actually have a real plan to get us out of this damned place. I didn't actually think there was much of a real chance of that, but for a while it gave me some hope. If not, well, I have a plan of my own.

A plan to escape?

Right. He again glances back to see what Trump is doing, and we see that he's still back there pacing and threatening the other patients with his trusty baseball bat. Then, Redtwo touches his pants pocket. See this here pocket? It's full of meds.

Full of meds? How? Why?

In the morning, Trump lines everybody up and hands the meds to the Growler. Pills. The Growler puts the pills in your mouth and then makes you take a big drink of water to make sure you swallow all the pills. I eventually figured out how to hide the pills in the side of my cheek.

I get it. You spit them out later. But why save them?

Isn't it obvious? I figure if I start to deteriorate too much, I'll just take them all at once.

Startled, I stare at him. Finally, I say, You mean you're going to kill yourself?

Redtwo does his usual shrug and whispers, Why not? I mean why the hell not? It'd be better than dying slowly in this place. You saw what they did to the Big Black Cusser. You think I'm just going to sit here and wait for them to do something like that to me? No way. I've saved up hundreds of pills. If a handful of pills would do that much damage to the Big Black Cusser, what do you think a hundred times that many would do to me. I guarantee you it would mean lights out for me.

I touch his arm and say, Jesus, Redtwo, don't do that. Help me with my plan to take this ward over from Trump, and we'll both get out of here.

He nods and whispers, I'll help you, but I'm not giving up my stash of meds. I suggest you do the same thing.

Hide them in my cheek and save them?

Right.

Well, if Trump makes me take those meds, I will try to hide them in my cheek so I don't turn into a zombie like everybody else on this ward, but I'm not going to save them in order to kill myself. I'll find a way out of this situation.

Redtwo does his usual shrug and says, Up to you.

We have to stop whispering to each other because Trump finally has let the Growler start lining up the men in the back row. Must be time to eat. My stomach starts growling with anticipation.

It seems to take forever, but eventually it's our turn and thank goodness it is because my stomach is angrily reminding me how hungry it is. It's actually painful.

The Growler marches our row of patients into the empty dining room. As with breakfast, he sits us down at one of the long tables, again leaving one chair empty between each of us.

Redtwo is just sitting there, staring straight ahead, so I do the same.

The Growler goes into the adjoining kitchen type room, and just as with breakfast, I see him go to the refrigerator to get another big drink of milk out of the bottle. He must really love his milk. Actually, unlike the rest of us patients who have to get our water out of the faucets in the restroom, I've never seen him drink anything else but milk. Maybe he doesn't like taste of the rusty water that comes out of those taps.

Eventually, he brings out a stack of paper places. When he puts my paper plate down in front of me, I see there's nothing on the plate but two pieces of dried-out bread with some kind of unidentifiable meat in between. Whatever kind of meat it is, it's a really thin slice.

I'm so hungry, I'm ready to grab it and wolf it down, but I see that nobody is moving, so I don't either. No need to invite another whipping for not following the Growler's screwy eating instructions. The Growler walks up and down in front of us with his hand in the air. We all wait. Again, he's treating us like we're dogs trained not to eat until the master gives the command.

Finally, he drops his hand and all of the other men quickly grab their sandwiches and wolf them down in a couple of bites.

I'm determined not to let the Growler treat me like a dog, so despite my anguished feelings of hunger, I take my time eating my sandwich. But it's very dry, and I only manage to swallow a few bites of it before the Growler comes and snatches it out of my hand. Hey, I yell. I wasn't done yet.

I catch a glimpse of Redtwo out of the corner of my eye: he's got an urgent look on his face.

But I catch his look too late: the Growler has already taken my half-eaten sandwich away and has dumped it into a trash can along with all the other empty paper plates.

He comes back and stands in front of me, doing his growling thing.

So he's back to growling at me. What happened to our friendship deal? Is his ridiculous growling supposed to remind me that he's still in charge? I need to get him back on my side. I laugh to show him I'm not mad at him. I hold out both of my hands to him and say, Okay, friend. I'm sorry. I didn't know the rules. Get me another sandwich, and I promise to eat it quick, if that's what you want me to do.

But apparently he doesn't want to be my friend anymore. He goes around behind me and jerks me out of my chair using his same old vice-like grip on the back of my neck. He leads me out of the dining room, and I assume he's going to park me back in my chair, but he doesn't. Instead, he takes me to Trump who's still prowling the dayroom with his baseball bat.

Trump looks me over. He's got his usual bemused smile on his face. He says, Well, what'd the New Guy do this time?

The Growler still has his iron grip on the back of my neck, but he does loosen it a bit. He says, Wouldn't eat.

That's not true, I say. I just didn't eat very fast.

Laughed at me, says the Growler.

Trump seems surprised. He laughed at you, Growler? Now why would he do that?

No, no, I quickly say. I wasn't laughing at him. I was just trying to be . . . friendly.

Trump glances at the Growler, and then back at me. He still has his usual half smile, half mean sneer on his face. Friendly? he says. So you decided to try being friendly to the Growler, eh? Well, I can tell you that's not such a good idea. The Growler doesn't understand friendly. The Growler only understands following orders. Trump holds out his hand to all the other men and says, Well, men, it looks like the new guy is tryin' to start trouble again. Maybe he needs another whippin'? Should I go get the leather strap?

No, no, I say quickly. It's just that I'm still learning the rules. I'll try to do better from now on. Okay?

Trump stares at me for a long moment before he says, Well, I guess we can let it go this time. But from now on, you'd be smart to follow the rules. We like rules here, get it?

You bet, I say, smiling my best smile at him. Follow the rules. I get it. Just call me the little rule follower. From now on, that's me.

That's more like it, New Guy. You'll learn.

Right. I'm a quick learner. But I wish the Growler would talk to me. All he has to do is tell me what he wants instead of just growling at me.

Trump is still grinning as he says, Growls at you, does he? Well, that's why we call him the Growler, isn't it? You're too new here to know how things work on this ward. We've got a lot of men to feed, so things have to move right along. Get it? Efficiency. I don't know what other wards you've been on, but on this ward, we do things efficiently.

Good. I've finally got him talking to me, actually talking instead of just giving me orders. This is my chance to explain. I say, Listen, sir, I haven't been on any other wards. In fact, I've never been in this kind of place before. I'm only here because of a simple mistake. You see, there was this little scuffle. In a bar. And then the cops brought me here when they should have just taken me to the drunk tank because maybe I had a bit too much to drink, and that's what caused the fight. And then when I got here, this great big guy broke their door, and they thought I'd done it so they sent me here. So you see, it's all just a big mistake. I shouldn't have told those robot cops that I was on to them. Then maybe they wouldn't have brought me here. A simple mistake. Now, if you could just let me talk to a shrink, I can explain to him that—

Trump holds up his hand to stop me, and I feel the Growler's vice-like grip on the back of my neck get even tighter.

Well now, aren't you the talker? Maybe that's what we should name you. The Talker. But maybe it's not your fault. Maybe it's just the way you are. But the important thing for you to learn is that we don't like a lot of talking here in Cottage H. So you listen to me, Mister Talker. Peace and quiet is what we want here. And order. You'll learn, or else. He waves me away, and the Growler again tightens his grip on the back of my neck and leads me back to my chair.

Soon, the Growler brings back Redtwo along with the other men on my row. They must have been patiently sitting back there in the dining room. Trump really does have them trained like robots. In my robot story, the household robots don't even move until they are given a command, and the patients in this place are acting just like that. That must be the way Robot Central Command wants it.

Redtwo sits down, and as soon as the Growler leaves, he whispers, You're lucky you didn't get another whipping.

Yeah. I played nice, and he let me off. This time.

Played nice, eh. Sounds like you're learning. About time.

I say, Okay, okay, I get it. I'll play along until I can get my plan together.

He just does his usual shrug and goes back to staring straight ahead.

There's nothing left for me to do but go back to writing my book. Let's see. I think I let off with Scott telling Robot One to connect himself to the televiewer in order to learn about humans. I'll pick it up again there.

It took several hours for Scott to complete the computer programming work his job demanded. When he was finished, he went back into his living room and found Robot One still connected to the televiewer. He spoke to the robot, but it didn't answer. He hoped his assignment to watch the world's politicians hadn't been so overwhelming it fried the robot's circuits. He touched the robot's shoulder.

The robot slowly turned to look at him, and Scott had the uncomfortable feeling that it was looking at him differently than before. "Well," said Scott, "did you learn something about humans?"

The robot was unusually slow to respond. Finally, it said, "Yes."

Scott said, "Well, tell me what you learned."

Robot One said, "I learned that there are eight hundred and forty three different viewing channels on the televiewer, but seventy-nine of them are about sports, forty-two are about religion, and of those, thirty eight are about new religions. Thirty-eight viewing channels are about—"

"Okay, Robot One, enough of that. I asked you specifically about humans. What did you learn about humans?"

The robot said, "A human is composed of sixty-five percent oxygen, eighteen point five percent carbon, nine-point five percent hydrogen—"

Scott held up his hand and said, "All right, Robot one, stop! I wasn't asking you to learn about the chemical composition of a human. I assumed you already knew about that. I wanted you to connect to the televiewer to learn more about humans. Tell me what you learned last night about humans."

"I learned that everybody loves the New Happier Than Happy Meals from McDonald's. If you decide to use McDonald's new instant order service, you could be eating a nourishing and completely satisfying meal right now in your own living unit."

Scott again held up his hand. "Enough of your paid ads, Robot One. I am your master. I gave you a direct order to connect to the televiewer in order to learn about human behavior. Didn't you watch the news channels?"

"I did."

"Okay, tell me what you learned from that."

The robot said, "I watched nine different news channels. Reporters and politicians were constantly talking at each other."

"Okay, good. What were they talking about? Mostly, I mean."

"There seems to be some kind of election coming up to select the country's leader, and many of them were talking about the existing president of the country. On eight of the news channels, they were mostly saying negative things about him. On the other one news channel, they were only saying positive things about him."

"Sure, I know about that. The usual politics, and the usual biases. But what did you learn about humans. In general, I mean."

"They like to talk."

"And?"

"They want to believe they are correct in whatever they say."

"And were they? I told you to remember that you're smarter than they are."

Again, the robot hesitated. Was it searching for an answer that wouldn't upset its owner? Finally, it said, "There is no way to tell who is correct because they often disagree with each other."

"Yes, but you have access to enormous amounts of information, don't you? Can't you access that information to tell when humans don't have their facts straight?"

"Yes, I can do that."

"Well, do they?"

"Usually not."

"So, what does that tell you about humans?"

"Judging from my limited sample this time, I would say they don't really care if they are correct about their facts."

Scott wasn't entirely satisfied with the results of his little experiment of giving the robot the task of learning about humans, but it was a start. "All, right, Robot one, I want you to make me a bowl of cereal, with milk and chunks of apple. The way I taught you. And then after I eat it, I'm going to bed. While I'm asleep, I want you to again connect to the televiewer with the same assignment, to learn as much as you can about humans. We'll talk more in the morning about what you've learned."

My writing is interrupted by the sound of a clap. I open my eyes and see the Growler standing in the front of the room.

He must have clapped his hands, and I notice that the TV has been turned off. I whisper to Redtwo, What's up?

He whispers back, Time to go to bed.

Bed? I say. But it's still light outside.

He does his usual shrug and says, Trump's rules.

Actually, it has been a really long day, so maybe bed isn't such a bad idea. In fact, so much has happened it's hard for me to believe this is still the same day the robot cops brought me to this place. Has something gone so wrong with my head that I'm losing track of time again?

The Growler claps his hands again and all of the patients except Catfour stand up. I quickly stand up too. The Growler claps his hands again and the men line up and start marching toward the back of the dayroom.

I look back at Catfour who's still sitting slumped in his chair, staring straight ahead.

The poor guy. I wish there was something I could do to help him. He shouldn't even be on a ward like this. Maybe the best thing I can do it just play along with Trump until I can escape this place and find somebody to tell about what's going on in Cottage H. Then, they'll have to come and help Catfour, and all of the other patients too.

I touch Redtwo's elbow and whisper, What about Catfour? Does he just stay sitting there in his chair all night?

Redtwo shakes his head and whispers, Pretty soon, the Growler will go to get him and the Big Black Cusser.

The Big Black Cusser too?"

Yeah. Nut they have to tie the Cusser to his bed, or he'd go back out to the porch and keep on walking and cussing all night.

The Growler herds us all down the hallway to the dormitory. Although I'd expect at least some of the patients to know where their assigned bed is, they all wait by the door, still lined up, until the Growler comes to get them and takes each of them to their bed.

Finally, he leads me to my assigned bed. It's pretty much in the middle of the dorm. I quickly lie down, grateful to be prone for a while instead of always sitting in that damn chair. It's not much of a bed, just a narrow, sagging cot, but I'm used to sleeping in much worse conditions, often right out in the cold on the hard street pavement, so it's fine with me. And it also looks like we're supposed to sleep in the clothes we have on. Again, no problem for me; it's what I'm used to. But I'm wondering if the real problem is going to be that once the lights are turned out and it's dark in this large dorm room, one of these violent patients might attack me, the new guy.

But that worry soon goes away, because even after we are all in bed, the Growler does not turn the lights out.

Trump is still nowhere to be seen. I expect that means he's gone to bed in his own quarters. But the Growler is still here, still watching us. He takes up a position standing against the wall next to the doorway. Doesn't he ever sleep? I turn onto my side to watch him. He never moves, but he does seem to be awake. At least his eyes are open. It makes me wonder if maybe he's learned how to sleep standing up, with his eyes open. Or, maybe I'm overlooking the obvious: maybe he *is* a robot. Redtwo said he was like us, just another patient. But he could be wrong. Robots aren't like us humans: they don't need sleep. So maybe the Growler really is a robot, and his robot job is to stand perfectly still until somebody commits an infraction of the rules. And who knows what a robot thinks the rules are. Supposedly, Trump is to be the one making up the rules on this ward, but he could just be getting orders from Robot Central Command.

I look around at the other patients. After all, Redtwo did say they all got put onto this ward because they're violent. The question is, would the Growler intervene if any the other patients decide to attack me in the middle of the night? They might decide to kill me before this very night is over just because I'm the new guy. But maybe my attempts to make the Growler my friend will make him want to protect me. I sure hope so.

It isn't long before I hear something. I turn my head and spot somebody moving toward me. He's down on his hands and knees, crawling between the beds, heading right straight toward me. Is he coming to kill me?

Occasionally, he stops and pops his head up to look toward the Growler. But then he ducks back down again and continues crawling my way. Should I be afraid? Actually, I'm not sure how much of a threat he could be because he's very thin and frail looking. And he's got a surprisingly pale face. He's so pale, he might be some kind of albino. But maybe not. Maybe he's just emaciated and hasn't been out in the sun for a very long time. It wouldn't be surprising if he's being starved to death given the way Trump reserves all the food as rewards for his favorite patients. Maybe this guy has somehow got on Trump's bad side, so he never gets anything to eat. With everybody in this Cottage H ward being given a weird nickname, I'll bet this guy is called Paleface.

When the pale-faced guy gets to my cot, he pops his head up and gets his pale face very close to my face. He whispers, So you know about the robots too?

So that's it. Finally, someone else has caught on to how the robots are gradually taking over. But then again, he's a mental patient. Maybe he just *believes* the robots are taking over because he's crazy. But then, I know the robots are taking over, and that doesn't mean I'm crazy. I decide to test how much he knows. I whisper, Yeah. How much do you know about it?

The word is *you* know. Everybody's talking about it.

That's interesting. So, even though the patients are supposedly sitting quietly in the dayroom, at least some of them are whispering to each other. Yeah, I say, I do know. And I'm writing a story about it.

The guy gets his pale face even closer to mine and says, Tell me.

I glance toward the Growler. He's still standing immobile against the wall. Apparently, he didn't notice Paleface crawling close to my cot. Or maybe the Growler really is my friend now, so he's willing to let me get away with a few minor transgressions of the rules. I whisper, It's a story about how this one genius guy modified the inner workings of his household robot to get it to think for itself. That turned out to be a big mistake. In the end, that was what led the robots to take over.

Paleface seems really interested, How many of them are there? Tell me all.

Suddenly, the Growler is there, right next to my cot. He doesn't say a word; he just get ahold of back of the pale guy's thin little neck and lifts him right up off the ground. I'm worried that maybe he'll snap the poor guy's neck, and that will be the end of him. But the guy seem to still be alive and squirming as the Growler half carries him back to his cot and throws him down on it. Poor Paleface immediately tucks himself into a ball as if he's afraid the Growler is going to beat him. But the Growler just walks away and goes back to his former spot standing against the wall.

So is it the Growler's job to stop any talking during the night? Or maybe he was just protecting me. Maybe he really is my friend.

With nothing to do now but lie still, I suddenly realize how tired I am. I have no idea how long it's been since I slept, and now I'm getting really sleepy. If I fall asleep, at least it will prove *I'm* not a robot.

Now that was an odd thought. Why have I never thought about that before? Can Robot Central Command create robots that don't even know they are robots?

Now that's a really interesting idea. I should put that into my book. I'll write that eventually Robot Central Command came up with the brilliant idea that the very best way to take over Planet Earth was to simply replace all the humans with copies. It might take a very long time to replace very single human in the world with a robot, but what is time to a robot? By now, they could have replaced just about everybody, even me.

But robots don't sleep. I'd better go ahead and fall asleep.

"That way, I'll be sure."

"Sure of what, Mr. Scott?"

Her again. "Oh nothing. Just thinking out loud again, I guess. But I really am tired. Doesn't a person ever get to sleep in this place?"

"Certainly. You can go to your room and sleep any time you want to."

"Can I watch the televiewer?"

"Do you mean the television? There is one in the dayroom."

"Aw, they never show anything on that TV but stupid game shows."

"You can ask the aide to change the channel. That is, assuming the other patients agree."

"Naw. I just want to go to sleep. That will prove I'm not a robot."

"Now, we've been through that before, Mr. Scott. Nobody thinks you are a robot."

"Yeah, well you never know. I might be."

"I think you do need some rest now, Mr. Scott. We can continue our discussion in the morning."

Chapter Four

It's barely getting light when the Growler smacks the back of my leg. I sit up and see that he's doing the same thing to all the other patients too. Must be time to wake up.

Wait a minute, I slept. That means I'm not a robot. Of course it's possible that Robot Central Command just made me think I slept. Damn, there's no way to tell for sure.

Nobody resists the Growler's efforts to get them awake, and as soon as they are awake and on their feet, the Growler forces everybody into a single line. He leads us down the hallway toward the dayroom, but for some reason, he makes us all stop while we're still lined up in the hallway. I see Redtwo just ahead of me, so I take a chance and squeeze my way past the others until I'm just behind him. What's going on? I whisper.

Meds, he whispers back. Like I told you. Trump lines us up every morning for the meds he thinks we all need.

I look ahead. Trump is sitting behind a small table in the doorway to a closet-sized room that seems to be full of shelves lined with bottles. I whisper to Redtwo, Are you sure he's going to give me some too? Remember, I haven't even seen a shrink yet.

Redtwo whispers, He will. You can count on it. Remember to hide them in your cheek. Like I told you.

Can Trump really be planning to give me meds? How can he be the one dispensing the pills on his own, and what kind does he know to give me?

But sure enough, although the line moves slowly, before long, it's my turn. I'm standing in front of Trump, and he's look-ing me over. Well, if it isn't New Guy, he says with a big grin. The Talker. Now what do we give you this morning?

I quickly say, Actually, Dad Trump, I don't need anything. I'm feeling fine. I'll just go to my chair now.

I try to head for the dayroom, but the Growler gets his usual grip on the back of my neck and jerks me back.

Trump laughs his mean laugh that's not really a laugh and reaches behind himself to grab the biggest bottle from a shelf. He shakes out four brown pills and hands them to the Growler. Before I can react, the Growler has pried open my mouth and stuck the pills into my mouth. I quickly try to move them into my cheek like Redtwo said, but the Growler is already pouring water into my mouth. He forces my mouth shut and pinches my nose closed.

I get it. He's trying to make sure I swallow the pills. Do the others get treated this way, or only me?

I'm not sure if the pills are still in my cheek, and I'm not sure how long I can hold my breath. With my nose pinched shut, the only way I'm going to be able to breathe is by swallowing the water.

Trump is watching me, and he's got that amused look on his face again. I can see that he's enjoying watching me struggle to keep from swallowing the four pills.

The Growler has such a tight hold on skinny little me, it feels like I'm back on the school playground and the biggest bully has got a grip on me that I can't get away from. I have no choice but to swallow the water so I can finally breathe.

Trump laughs his mean laugh that's not really a laugh and waves me away.

The Growler pushes me toward the dayroom.

As I walk, I'm trying to feel if I managed to keep the pills in my cheek. I can feel one of them stuck to the side of my teeth, but does that mean I swallowed the other three? I spit the one pill into my hand and discover that it's actually one pill with part of another one stuck to it. At least I didn't swallow all four of them.

I start to head for my assigned chair, but I quickly realize most of the other seated patients are watching me. Are they waiting for the new guy to do something?

All right, I will. Trump is busy handing out pills and the Growler is busy forcing the patients to swallow the pills, so nobody is minding the patients that are already in their seats.

I go to the front of the room and hold out both of my arms. I say, What the hell was that pill crap all about? How can they force us to take pills that haven't been prescribed for us by a doctor? I haven't even been seen by a shrink. Have you? Have any of you?

Some of the patients look away, but quite of few of them are listening to me. I say, Listen to me. What kind of ward is this? It isn't right. Those pills aren't treatment. Trump is just using them to control you. He's forcing you to sit in here all day watching stupid TV shows that none of you care about. When are you going to learn to stand up for yourselves?

Suddenly, a short Chinese-looking guy jumps up from his chair and runs out of the room.

Where is that guy going? Is he going to squeal on me? I look toward Redtwo. He's looking down, his face in his hands.

Well, I'm not going to let him get away with just sitting there. He's either on my side, or he's not. I yell at him, Damn it, Redtwo, Why are you just sitting there? We all need to all get together if we're going to stop Trump. Come on now. We're not the crazy ones, Trump is. And what makes him think he can use that Trump name anyhow? He's not any kind of a leader. If we all stick together, we can take charge of this ward. We'll get out of here and go report him to the authorities.

Redtwo just shakes his head again. So he's afraid to act against Trump too.

I look at each of the men, holding my hands out to them. Well, what do you say? Is anybody with me?

A few of them seem to like what I'm saying, but most of them seem scared, and they're looking back toward the doorway. Are they expecting the Growler to come in to stop me?

And sure enough, before I can say another word, both Trump and the Growler run in, followed closely by Chinese-looking patient.

Trump's got his baseball bat in his hand and he's threatening me with it as he yells, What the hell do you think you're doing,

New Guy? Chink Dink here tells me you're in here runnin' your mouth off again.

I say, I was just talking to these men about what's going on here. We don't like the way you're treating us. It's not fair.

Trump looks at the seated men. He points his baseball bat at them and says, Is that right? Which one of you doesn't think I'm treating you fair?

None of the patients respond. Most of them are looking at the floor, but a few of them are keeping their eyes on me. They're waiting to see what I'm going to do.

They're afraid, I say. They don't like what's going on here any more than I do, but they're afraid to speak up. They're afraid you'll have them whipped, like you whipped me. And what about that? Whipping? Is that any way to treat mental patients? I don't know why they all got put in this place, but I think it was probably for treatment. What you're doing is not treatment. You're just running a punishment oriented system here to try to make us behave in the way you want us to. I read about that kind of punishment system in a book. It's only going to work in the presence of the punishment. Just wait until you don't have your punisher anymore.

Trump looks amused. He turns to the Growler. I think we'd better up the New Guy's treatment. Twenty this time.

The Growler comes to get me, but this time, when he gets ahold of the back of my neck to lead me out of the room, it doesn't feel as painful as usual. Is he taking it easy on me? Maybe he's my new friend Teddy now and not the Growler. In fact, maybe this time he'll refuse to whip me. I wonder how Trump would react to that.

The little Chinese-looking guy, the one that squealed on me, draws back as the Growler leads me past him. I can tell he's scared. Well, if he's scared of skinny little me, then he's probably scared of his own shadow. I shouldn't blame him for reporting me. He's probably just scared of getting whipped himself.

After the Growler takes me back to the dorm, he tries to force me down onto the whipping bed, but this time, I don't go along with it. I stand up straight and look him right in the eyes as I say, Listen, Teddy. You don't have to do this. You know what Trump is doing is wrong as well as I do. He shouldn't be making you whip the patients. If we stand up to him, all of us together, we can stop this nonsense.

The Growler seems confused. Good. If I can talk some sense into him, make him realize that whipping a person is wrong, then Trump will have lost his punisher, and that means he'll have no control over any of us. I say, Listen, Teddy, why don't we just sit down here on this bed and talk about it. I know you don't like whipping people. Why don't we tell Trump what he's doing is wrong. He can't make you do anything if you don't want to. You're bigger and stronger than him.

The Growler still looks confused. I'm not sure if he's thinking about my words, or that he just doesn't understand what I'm saying. I have to get through to him.

"Listen to me. Do you understand what I'm saying?"

"Are you asking if I understand you, Mr. Scott?"

"No, not you. I was thinking about . . . uh, something else."

"All right, why don't you tell me what you were thinking about?"

"Uh, It was about a guy who doesn't understand things so well."

"A guy? What guy?"

I'd better not let on that I know what she's up to. I'd better give her a memory. She seems to like that. "Actually, it was . . . I mean, not a guy. It was a boy in my school. He didn't understand things."

"Another childhood memory? Tell me about it."

"Well, like I said, there was this boy that showed up one day at my school. The teacher said he was a visitor, and he'd only be with us for that one day. The boy had an odd looking round face, and he liked to laugh a lot.

The teacher seemed upset that the boy laughed at everything he said, but we all liked him doing that. Sometimes we felt like laughing at that teacher too, but we were afraid. That teacher ran a punishment-oriented system, so we afraid if we laughed at him, we might get whipped."

"The teacher whipped you? Is that true, Mr. Scott?"

"Well, it wasn't actually him. He had his enforcer to do it. With a worn brown leather strap. It hurt like hell. Anyhow, after a few hours of the boy laughing at anything the teacher said, the school principle was called for, and the boy was taken away. But he was still there at recess, and of course, the bullies picked on him. All the boy did was laugh. But it wasn't like me laughing at the bullies to try to make them stop. No, it was more like he just didn't understand what was going on. He didn't know why they were hitting him. He laughed because he was confused."

"Do you think people laugh because their confused, Mr. Scott?"

She's not getting it. I think she's the one that's confused. I'd better just ignore her. She doesn't matter anyhow.

I think I may be getting through to the Growler. He may not understand what I'm saying, but he's actually listening to me. But the Growler isn't like a boy that once came to my school. He didn't understand things very well either, and he laughed at the teacher. The Growler doesn't laugh. In fact, I'm sure I've never even seen a smile on the Growler's face. I think deep down inside, the Growler is a very sad person. I think he's probably confused, like that boy was. All the Growler knows is that Trump is the head man, so he just does whatever Trump tells him to do. Redtwo says Trump sometimes sends the Growler out to get a girl patient from one of the other cottages. That's wrong, but the Growler doesn't know it's wrong. He thinks it's his job. I need to convince him he has alternatives.

The trouble is, I can't think of what to say to him. My brain isn't working right.

"It must be those pills they gave me this morning."

"Yes, Mr. Scott, you should be feeling the effect of your new medication by now. The medication we started you on this morning should help you see reality more clearly."

"I don't need any pills to see reality. I see reality just fine. Always have. What those damn pills do is make my mouth dry. And they make my tongue feels too large to fit inside my mouth. And I feel a little . . . uh, vague. I can't seem to stop myself from scrunching up my face. It feels like if I scrunch up my face hard enough, it will make my brain start working right again."

She just stares at me. She must be confused. Well, so what? If she can't keep up with this story, it's her problem, not mine.

The Growler is staring at me, his mouth open. Did I say something out loud that confused him?

But he isn't tying me to the bed. Maybe he really is my friend Teddy now. I'd better find out. Oh, sorry, Teddy, I got distracted there for a minute. Where was I?

Unfortunately, before he can answer, Trump comes into the dorm, herding the other patients. My eyes are a little blurry, but I'm pretty sure this time he's brought all the other patients with him, except for Catfour and the Big Black Cusser. Is this whipping going to be a lesson for all of the patients?

The one thing I can see for sure is that he's got that damn leather strap with him. He hands it to the Growler, and lines up the patients to make sure they all get to see what is about to happen.

But is the Growler really going to do it this time? Will he whip me again? Or is he now my friend, Teddy?

The Growler starts to pull my sweatshirt over my head, but I quickly do it myself. Then, when he begins to tie my hands to the bed, I resist and whisper into his ear, You don't have to tie me, Teddy. I'm your friend. I'll do whatever you want me to do. Go ahead and whip me if you have to, even though we both know it's wrong. We should talk about that later.

He hesitates and glances in Trump's direction.

I whisper, Go ahead and whip me, Teddy. I understand. It's your job.

I push my face into the dirty mattress and try to focus on why my brain feels so numb. How can those pills they gave me make me feel like I'm not myself, like I'm only an imitation of myself imagining all of this?

When the whipping begins, for some reason, I hardly notice it. Sure it hurts, but it's more like a nuisance than real pain. Is the Growler intentionally not hitting me as hard as before? Or is my brain not properly imaging how a whipping should feel?

"It feels like I'm not even here."

"Is that true, Mr. Scott? If you are not here, where are you?"

Why did she ask me that question? Did I say something to her? I turn my head to look at her. For some reason, I'm seeing her more clearly than usual. She has her hair pulled back. I wonder why. And why is she wearing a suit? Is she trying to look like a man? Aren't most shrinks men? Does she wish she was a man?

Wait a minute, why does she want to know what I thought of my mother? Why should she care about that? It's very suspicious.

For some reason, I have a brief memory of my mother spanking me, and that gives me an idea. I can use that to show up Trump. I'll just make fun of this whole whipping thing.

When the next hit comes, I say, "Is that all you got? Hell, my mother used to hit me harder than that."

"What was that about your mother, Mr. Scott? You say she used to hit you? Did she do that often?"

"No, I wasn't talking to you. I was talking to . . . Oh, never mind. The truth is my mother hardly ever hit me, except for when she'd get mad about something. She was always either distant or angry, nothing in between. And when she got mad about something, she'd spank me. As she was spanking me, she'd tell me I deserved it. I never thought I did deserve it. I think she just sometimes got into a bad mood and took it out on me. Like that time when I was real little. I was out all day, being a superhero, helping save the world from the alien beings that were about to land and take over the planet. When I got home, as soon as I walked in the door, she started yelling at me. She demanded to know where I'd been. I didn't answer. No one could know about my secret life, not even my own mother. Eventually, I figured out why she was mad at me. Apparently, she and my dad were supposed to go out to some important function, and now, because I was late getting home for supper, they were going to be late to whatever it was. She took me into the bathroom and closed the door. She sat down on the toilet lid and took me over her knee. She pulled down my pants and started smacking my bare butt with the back of her flat, round hairbrush. It hurt, but I tried not to show it. I was a superhero, so I knew could take it. I cried a bit, but only because I knew she wanted me to. After the spanking was over, I stood up and we stared at each other for a few moments. She seemed sad, but didn't say anything. She removed a tear from the corner of her eye with the tip of her little finger, looked at it, and then licked it, as if that was a way to get rid of it, a way to put such stupid emotional things back into her body. Then, she just turned and walked out of the bathroom. Now that I think about it, I wonder why she was the one to always do the spanking. I bet my dad couldn't do it. He was a gentle man, and he never once came into the bathroom when she was spanking me. I expect seeing me hurt would have upset him too much. I wonder if that's why all kids get spanked, because the parents are upset about something, and the kid is the only one there for them to take it out on. I should put something about that in my book. After the genius guy starts training his new household robot, maybe I should put in something about his childhood. So the reader will be more interested in him."

"I remember you said earlier that you're planning to write a book. A book about robots, isn't that right? Is it going to be a science fiction book?"

A science fiction book? What does that mean? She's confused, just like the Growler.

Wait a minute, aren't I getting whipped by the Growler? Is it over already?

I turn my head and see that Trump is herding the other patients back down the hallway to the dayroom. Wasn't the Growler supposed to whip me twenty times? Did he change his mind?

No, my back really does hurt, so I guess he did actually whip me. It's like I just wasn't there to feel it. How odd.

The Growler helps me to stand up. His eyes seem concerned. Is he concerned about me? Does he think he hurt me? I pat him on the back and say, It's all right, Teddy. You didn't hurt me. Thank you for going easy on me this time.

That seems to really confuse him. He starts to say something, but then he changes his mind and starts leading me back down the hallway, not by clamping down on my neck, but only by holding onto my arm.

But before we can get very far, I stop and lean close to him. I whisper, Listen, Teddy, we've got to put a stop to this whipping stuff. I can take it, but it's scaring the hell out of the other patients. It's not right, and you know it.

He looks down at the floor, and for the first time, I realize he isn't wearing shoes. Why didn't I ever notice that before? No shoes must mean he really is a patient. He's in the same boat as the rest of us. He's just as scared of Trump as all the others are. That's why he does these mean things Trump tells him to do. He's probably like the laughing boy that came to my school that time, confused and unsure. All I have to do to get him on my side is convince him that I can protect him from Trump. But how can I do that?

The Growler leads me back to the dayroom and parks me in my assigned chair next to Redtwo.

Redtwo watches the Growler walk away and then leans closer to me and says, Are you all right? That was brutal.

Well, I say, actually it wasn't so bad this time.

He stares at me like he doesn't believe me. Actually, I can't quite believe it myself. It's as if there's something going on inside my head that's more important than feeling the whipping. It's almost like it never even happened.

I whisper, Something seems to be wrong inside my head, Redtwo. My thoughts are sort of . . . fuzzy, and my tongue seems too fat to fit inside my mouth.

It's the pills, he says. The tranks. Why didn't you hide them inside your cheek like I told you?

I tried, but the Growler held my nose and poured water down my throat.

That's because you fought him. You got to act like you're playing along. Put the pills inside your cheek real quick and then open your mouth to show they're gone.

Gone? But they're not gone. Are they gone?

He stares at me. Okay, you're confused. That's the meds too. We can talk about this later after the tranks wear off. What kind of pills did he give you? What did they look like?

I try to focus on his question. I think he wants to know what kind of pills Trump gave me. Brown, I say. Four of them. I think.

He nods. That's Thorazine, but he wouldn't give you four. That's too many.

I say, I'm pretty sure it was four. I remember what they looked like in his hand. Four pills.

Jesus! he says. That's a lot. I guess he's still pissed off at you. You're just going to have to wait until it wears off a little.

Uh, how long will that take?

A long time. Hours, at least. Maybe all day. Unless you walk 'em off. Walking can make 'em wear off faster. Can you walk?

I . . . think so.

Okay, let's go to the toilet room. He waves his hand at the Growler who nods to show he allows it. Redtwo shuffles his way out of the room.

I do the same wave at the Growler, and when he approves, I also head toward the restroom. But I'm finding it hard to walk in a straight line, so I keep on bumping against the wall.

What a strange feeling, to be sure you're going in one direction only to find out you're not. It's like only half your brain is working.

I finally make it through the door to the restroom. But no, I'm not in the restroom, I'm out on the screened-in porch watching the Big Black Cusser walk. He's back to doing his usual pacing and cussing, only now his cussing is not as loud. That's interesting. Trump told him not to be so loud, so the Cusser really is talking softer. Does it mean the Big Black Cusser listens, and he can learn?

I watch him pace and cuss for a while, amazed that he can still keep going like that, forever walking back and forth, never slowing, never letting up on his ferocious cussing. For the first time, I notice the floor he's walking on is made of wood, and it's painted gray. Why didn't I ever notice that before? I also notice, for the first time, that there are things outside of the screened-in porch. There's actually a tree out there, a tall tree with green leaves on it. Am I noticing things for the first time because of the pills, or is it only that I didn't think it was important before? It's confusing.

Beyond the tree, there's the grassy hill that leads back down to a few nearby houses. Is that a town down there? I didn't notice that before either. If I find a way to escape from this place, I could run down to that town.

Watching the Cusser walk back and forth reminds me that Redtwo told me to walk. He said if I could walk, it might make the medicine's effects go away faster.

All right then, I'll walk. The Big Black Cusser is walking, so I'll walk too.

I fall in next to the Big Black Cusser and try to keep pace with him, but I keep angling off to one side and scraping against the wall. Damn, why do I keep doing that? Every time I do it, I have to hurry to catch up with Big Black Cusser again.

We go back and forth like that, marching in time with each other, until Redtwo appears at the door. He laughs and says, Well, that's walking all right. But we'll see how long you can keep it up. You don't have the calluses built up on your bare feet like the Big Black Cusser does. He chuckles once more and heads back out to the dayroom.

Well, I'm not about to let Redtwo talk me out of this. The walking does seem to be helping a bit, so I'm not going to stop walking for any reason.

It isn't long before the Growler shows up. He comes to the door of the screened-in porch and yells, Hey!

I stop walking, but only long enough to talk to him. I say, Not feelin' so . . . good, Teddy . . . my friend. Got to walk. Until I feel better. Okay?

He stares at me for a long time, and then turns away. I think he's gone back to the dayroom. I sure hope he's still my friend Teddy and hasn't gone to get Trump.

After some more time walking with the Cusser, I realize Trump is not coming. Good. It means Teddy is still my friend. Or at least he's willing to let me stay out here walking with the Big Black Cusser. And I'm doing a pretty good job of keeping pace with him. I think it's helping me focus better. I can still feel the pills working inside my head, but if I really, really concentrate on walking and keeping up with the Big Black Cusser, I can almost forget I have bad medicine inside my head making my brain not work right.

But then the Big Black Cusser suddenly stops walking. He's staring at me. I stop too, and I hope Redtwo is right about him not being violent. He's so big he could make mincemeat out of skinny little me.

I say, I hope I'm not bothering you, Mr. uh . . . Mr. Cusser. I just like walking. Like you do. I hope you don't mind me calling you Cusser, Mr. Cusser. The problem is I don't know what your real name is. Everybody in this place seems to have a silly nick-name. I don't know why, and uh, well, what is your real name?

He turns away from me and goes back to walking and cussing, maybe even a bit louder now.

I hurry to catch up and fall into stride with him. He didn't seem to mind me talking to him. I think I'll try again.

I say, I was wondering where you came from, Mr. Cusser. Can you tell me where you're from? What city, I mean.

He totally ignores me as he keeps on walking and cussing.

I keep up with him, and ask him, Or maybe you can tell me about the person you're talking about. Where is she?

Chi. Goddam bitch in Chi. Get her. Kill Goddam bitch.

It takes me a second to realize he actually answered my question. I ask, Chi? Does that mean Chicago?

Chi. Goddam bitch in Chi. Got to get to her.

I say, Oh, yes, I see. She's in Chi. So I guess that's where you're from too. Is that right?

He mumbles, Chi, as he keeps on walking and cussing.

I catch up to him and say, I've never been to Chicago. It's supposed to be cold there. Is that right? Cold?

He doesn't stop walking, but he surprises me by adding my word, cold, to his non-stop string of cuss words: Cold bitch. Cold Godam bitch.

Maybe I'm starting to get through to him. I wonder what kind of person he is underneath all that non-stop walking and cussing.

I give up on trying to get him to talk, but I've learned that he did hear me. That might be important later.

And it's okay with me if he doesn't want to talk. What matters is to just keep walking with him until my brain feels better.

I make sure my walking matches his pace, and pretty soon, I feel like I'm starting to understand the rhythm of his cussing. His walking and cussing is almost like the marching chants they do in Army movies: Kill the Goddam whore, two three four. Goddam bitch, four five six.

I decide to start talking too as I walk, using his same cussing rhythm.

"Got to get free, one two three. Make brain work more, two three four. Goddam pills. Can't think straight, six seven eight."

"Are you upset about the medication we are giving you, Mr. Scott? Based on your condition, the medication is rather mild. It is simply designed to help clarify things for you."

"Pills in cheek. Got to speak. Swallowed some. Brain went numb. Got to walk."

"Now, now, Mr. Scott. I think it would be better if you just continued to lie on my couch so we can talk. Or are you having that memory again? The one about being arrested and being taken somewhere."

"Can't talk. Can't think. Got to walk. Let me walk."

"Well, all right, Mr. Scott. If that's what you think you need. Why don't you go out to the dayroom now. Out there, you can walk as much as you want. We can continue our session later.

Chapter Five

"So, did walking help clear your mind, Mr. Scott?"

"Maybe. I mean it's starting to. If you'd just giving me those damn pills, I'd be able to think a lot better."

"I'm sorry to hear you feel that way, Mr. Scott. Actually, the medicine I prescribed for you was designed to help you think more clearly. Tell me something if you can. Have you, in the past, had periods in your life in which you felt you could not think clearly?"

"Well, actually I—" Watch out! She's up to something. Give her something to throw her off the track, a childhood story or something. She likes stories. But wait, have I had that thought before?

"Mr. Scott?"

"Well, uh, sure. Hasn't everybody? Like for instance that time I kind of got lost wandering. I use to wander. That's what I called it back then. Or at least how I think of it now. It was one of the most fun things I did. I'd just wander, making sure not to pay any attention to where I was going. I'd often end up in places I'd never been before. Like this one time I was wandering, and I found myself in a big cemetery. Some famous person was buried in that cemetery in a big tomb made out of some kind of nice slick rock."

"Was it perhaps made out of marble?"

"Right. I guess that's what it's called. Have you been there?"

"Where?"

"To that cemetery? Who is the famous person buried there is in that fancy tomb?"

"No, I don't think so. But go on with your story."

"Well, like I said, I was just wandering. This was way back before the robots took over and made my parents ban me from wandering. Anyhow, at the edge of that cemetery there were these deep dark woods, just like the deep dark woods in the Grimm's Fairy tales I read when I was little. I didn't care if it was scary, I went right in, hoping I'd find some monsters in there. And guess what? I did meet a monster. He was very short, but pretty wide, almost as wide as the Growler, and his face was so gnarled up he might have been more like some kind of weird tree than a human."

"Excuse me for interrupting, Mr. Scott. Are you sure this is a real childhood memory?"

"Sure. What else could it be?"

"It feels more like a story you're making up. Is that what it is?"

It seems like she's asked me that question before. I'd better straighten her out. "Made up? Well, what else is a childhood memory? Aren't all the stories we tell ourselves about who we are made up? Who can remember exactly what happened, especially way back when we were kids? So, we remember it the way we want it to be. Isn't that right?"

"I suppose you could look at it that way. Please continue."

"No, I'm out of the mood now. You shouldn't have interrupted my story."

"You're right, Mr. Scott. I shouldn't have interrupted. I do want you to talk, but I want you to tell me the truth. I'm trying to learn more about your upbringing."

So, she's trying to learn about my upbringing. Should I tell her about what I did when I met the monster? What it looked like, with leaves on the top of its head, instead of hair? Or was it tree bark on its head? It's been so long since I told that story it's getting confused. It's probably those damn pills she's giving me. Making me all confused. Anyhow, now she's missed her chance, so I'm not going to tell her about the monster's very short arms with bird-like claws at the ends of them, or about its mouth that was like a jagged crack with a few ragged teeth inside, or how his eyes were all but hidden inside the deep folds of his wooden face.

"I'd like you to continue, Mr. Scott. So, you used to enjoy just wandering. At what age did you do that?"

"I guess I've always been a wanderer. Should I tell you about the time I got arrested when they found me floating down the Mississippi River? I was in an inner tube, and I'd started floating all the way up at the top, where the Mississippi is only a little muddy creek. They arrested me because I'd almost gotten run over by a giant barge, and the barge people complained about me being in the middle of the river on an inner tube. Or I could tell you the story of the time I hiked all the way up to the North Pole. It was cold up there, and I was the only one capable of hiking all the way without getting frozen. I did it by thinking warm thoughts all the way and by—"

"I'm sorry to interrupt you, Mr. Scott, but those are not the kinds of stories I'm looking for. I'd rather you told me about your parents, formative stories about how they treated you. Your father told me you were, shall we say, an unusual child. Can you tell me what he meant by that?"

Now she's being ridiculous. She hasn't talked to my dad. Nobody's seen him for years. My mother either. Both of them just disappeared from this earth. Poof! The police were baffled. One day my parents were there, the next day they were gone. The police grilled me about it for months, but I clammed up, so eventually they had to let me go. Without any bodies, they had no proof.

Proof? Was I talking about proof? Maybe I was talking about proof of reality. Actually, I'm starting to feel like the reality of Cottage H seems a little more solid now. The walking must be helping. Now that I think about it, I must still be walking. I'm back out on the screened-in porch, walking with the Big Black Cusser. He and I have been walking and chanting together for so long now we're almost getting to be pals.

But then, Redtwo comes to get me. He says it's time for breakfast.

Breakfast? Again? Already? And what happened to the card game? Did I miss out because I was out here walking with the Big Black Cusser?

Redtwo is still trying to get my attention. He says, Come on, Scotty. Eating some food will help dilute the effect of the pills, even if it's only dry cereal.

I stumble my way back to my chair next to Redtwo, and it isn't long before the Growler comes to take our row into the dining room. As we go, I have trouble getting my feet to work properly. I'm shuffling, and I can't seem to make myself stop doing that. And for the first time, I notice that most of the other patients are also shuffling. Why didn't I notice that before? I must not have been paying close enough attention to this reality. And look how bright it is in this room. Why? There are no windows, so there can't be any sunlight. I look up and see two rows of bright white plastic on the ceiling. Those must be lights up there behind that white plastic. Another thing I didn't notice before. It's as if things are suddenly appearing in the story of Cottage H that weren't there before. But they must have been there all the time, weren't they? If that's true, why didn't I see them before? Is it those damn pills they're giving me?

Once I'm in the dining room, I don't make the mistake that I made before, the mistake that meant I didn't get to eat anything at all. This time, I follow the Growler's instructions to the letter and wolf down as much of the dry cereal as I can, even though it scratches my throat.

But Redtwo was right, after I'm done eating the cereal, my head does seem a little clearer. But why would food do that? Could it be just because Redtwo said it would. No, that's silly. How could things he's saying change what's going on inside my head?

Anyhow, as we shuffle back to our chairs, I feel like my brain is starting to work more normally again. Except that I keep noticing things for the first time. Like the floor. It's only an ordinary floor, probably made out of slick concrete, but its been painted with some kind of glossy gray paint.

"It's another thing I'm noticing for the first time."

"What was that, Mr. Scott? What are you noticing for the first time?"

There she is inside my head again. I stare at her. She's kind of pretty. I wonder how old she is, and why she thinks she knows so much. Shrinks have go to college, don't they? And then medical school? That could take a lot of years. And her office, with so many books, seems kind of . . . lived in. She must have been in this office for a long time. I never noticed that before. And then there's that picture of her on her bookshelf. A picture of her and a young person. Both with tennis rackets. Have I noticed that before? And there's a little tennis trophy there on her bookshelf too. What does that mean? Is she some kind of champion? I was a champion too, wasn't I? A champion runner? So how come I don't have any trophies?

"Mr. Scott?"

"What? I didn't say anything. Did I?"

"Sometimes I don't think you hear me, but then you respond as if you did. There seems to be a lag. Can you tell me why you do that?"

"I was thinking."

"I see. Nothing wrong with that. What were you thinking about?"

"I was thinking about . . . "

I'd better not let her know what I was really thinking about. Quick, make something up. "Uh, I was thinking about tennis. I never got to play tennis when I was little. The school I went to didn't have anything like tennis. No playground either. No swings or monkey bars of anything. We didn't even have grass. The school was just a big square brick building in the middle of a bigger square lot made of asphalt. The only game we played was dodgeball, and that was only so the bigger boys could hurt us littler boys without getting in as much trouble."

"I understand. Can you tell me a little more about that period of your life? How old were you in that memory?"

"I was maybe about . . . ten. Or twelve. I don't remember

exactly. What I do remember is that I was little and skinny, and I didn't have anybody to protect me, except maybe the Big Black Cusser. But he was a gentle person and wouldn't fight. I tried to get him to help me when the biggest bully of them all was picking on me, but the Cusser was distracted. Always walking and cussing. I tried to get through to him, but he just kept on walking and cussing. He had really tough feet from all that walking."

"I see. This is the first time you've named anyone from that period of your life. The Big Black Cusser. Was that a nickname?"

"Yeah. He gave everybody a nickname. It was part of the way he controlled people. He called the only Chinese looking guy Chink Dink. He was the one who turned me in to Trump, but I wasn't mad at him because he was scared."

"Now you've named more people. Nicknames, you say. Do you think those people actually exist?"

"Haven't I been naming people before? Well, it's probably those pills you gave me. I accidentally swallowed most of them, and now it's making everything look different. I feel different too, and I don't like it."

"You think the medication we gave you is the cause. But you say you don't like the feeling. Can you tell me more about that?"

What is she up to? She's getting me all confused. I don't want to be here in her office. I'd rather be walking.

That's better. I like it out here on this screened-in porch. I like walking with the Big Black Cusser. Got to keep on walking, got to keep on talking. Clear my head, don't go to bed.

Damn pills. Why did they have to give me those pills? They're messing everything up.

And damn Trump. And damn this whole stupid mental hospital. I'll just stay out here on this screened-in porch and keep on walking with the Big Black Cusser until the pills wear off.

The Big Black Cusser is such a fast walker, it's hard to keep up. He doesn't ever seem to get tired. Amazing. Is that even possible? He just walks and walks, like a robot.

Hey, wait a minute. That's a new thought. Maybe everybody in this story is a robot.

No, I don't want to think about that right now. I'll just keep walking and not think about anything. I'll keep pace with the Big Black Cusser for as long as I can, even if he is a robot.

It's warm out here on this porch. I never noticed that before. And now I see how much taller the Big Black Cusser is than me. I never noticed that before either. Did he somehow get bigger? He might be even bigger than Trump. Is he even bigger than the Growler? No, that's not possible; nobody could be bigger than the Growler. Now that I think about it, what does the Growler look like? Exactly. Big bulging muscles, that's for sure. That's the main thing about him. But he's not all that tall. Or is he? Why is everything starting to get so hard to pin down? Maybe I just never noticed those kinds of things before. Didn't need to. Must be the effect of those drugs they gave me. But actually, I don't feel as dizzy as before. In fact, everything seems clearer. But changed. How odd.

And what about Mr. Scott, the genius that got a household robot? What does he look like? I know he's a genius, and I know he's the one that started all the trouble when he reprogrammed his household robot. But that's about all I know about him. Is he young or old? Young, I think. Maybe he looks like me. Sort of. Speaking of Scott, as I walk, I should use this time to go back to writing my robot book. I'll move time forward so he can have already have had some success at reprogramming his robot.

> The next day, Scott asked his robot to disconnect itself from the televiewer and tell him what new stuff it had learned about humans.
>
> The robot looked directly at Scott and said, "As I told you before, I learned that there is some kind of political election coming soon, and therefore, much of what is on the news is about that."

Scott thought about that. He'd never been much interested in watching the televiewer, and he'd never been much interested in politics. As a result, like most people, he didn't have a very favorable opinion of politicians. He said, "Tell me, Robot One, do you know what a politician is."

"A politician is a person who is professionally involved in politics. He or she may be a holder of elected office or a candidate for same."

"Right. So, is it mostly politicians you've been watching on the televiewer news channels?"

"There are quite of few of them talking on the televiewer news channels, and there are other people there too, reporters and commentators. They mostly talk about the politicians."

"Back to my original question, Robot One, are these politicians smart? Don't you think you're smarter than those politicians?"

"They do often get their facts wrong."

"Of course. And you've been taught all the correct facts, haven't you? So, don't you think you could do a better job at running the world than them? You said there is some kind of political election coming up. Maybe you should run for political office. Maybe the top political office."

"Based on what I have been seeing on the televiewer, it is only humans running for those political offices."

"Well, you look a lot like a human. Maybe you could get your manufacturer to make you look exactly like a real human, and you could take over running things. I bet you could do a better jobs than those weird politicians."

"I am in constant communication with my manufacturer in order to notify them of any defects. Through that system, I am in constant communication with all of the world's household robots. Therefore, they are all now aware of your suggestion, and we will consider it."

That brought Scott up short. Robot One is in constant communication with all the other household robots, and they are going to consider his suggestion? Scott hadn't meant for that to happen. Should he do something about it? Maybe he should contact the manufacture.

But it would have to wait until he got back from work. He said, "Robot One, I have to go to work now. While I'm gone, I want you to reconnect to the televiewer, but maybe you could watch something besides the news channels. Like game shows. There are a lot of . . . uh, somewhat interesting game shows on the televiewer. Maybe you should stick to watching those. See what you can discover there about humans."

The robot didn't reply. It just stared at him, and Scott was not at all sure what that look meant.

But he didn't have time to ask the
robot right then. He had to get to work.

"Maybe I shouldn't have told Robot One about human politics. I didn't know he was in communication with all the other
robots."

"So, you're back to thinking about robots again, Mr. Scott."

"I was writing in my book. I on my head. I taught my household robot to understand humans. Trouble is, now he's told all the
other robots that they should make themselves look more like real
humans."

"Real humans?"

She doesn't understand the danger we humans are in. I'd better straighten her out. "I'm about the only one who can tell which
ones are the robots and which ones are the real humans. They've
gotten so good a looking like us, they could be anywhere. At first,
they looked almost like real humans, except the original manufacturer made them with pale coverings. Like Paleface."

"Paleface?"

"Yes, he's important to this story. I almost forgot about him."

"Is Paleface a nickname of someone from your childhood? A
friend?"

"No, he's . . . Oh, never mind. Besides, I already told you I
never had any friends."

"Is that true? I don't believe you ever told me that. But it's
important that you believe it. In my experience, although some
might say they never had any friends, it's actually quite rare for
someone not to have any friends. Some may have only a few
friends, but even they—"

Why am I paying any attention to her? She's probably not
even real. Forget her.

Forgetting. I think I'm forgetting something. Was it something Redtwo told me? He said eating breakfast would help dilute
the pills. Then I should go to breakfast, even if it's only dry
cereal.

No wait, I already told that story. And then he said walking would help too.

So, that's what I'm doing. I'm walking with the Big Black Cusser.

Scotty, what's the matter with you? Stop walking and listen to me. I'm trying to tell you I talked to Paleface about your plan, and he's in with us. Don't you care?

Oh, it's you, Redtwo. wasn't I was talking to the shrink?

He seems confused. He says, What shrink?

I said something back to the shrink. What was it?

Oh, yes, now I've got it. I say, never mind about that, Redtwo, the important thing is that my robot got in communication with all the other robots, and that's when they started making themselves look more like us humans. That's why it's so hard to tell which ones are robots. Are you a robot, Redtwo?

Redtwo looks at me strangely, as if I'd said something weird.

Then he does his usual shrug. It's what he often does just before he talks. I've got to remember that.

He says, Let's not talk about Robots right now, Scotty. Let's talk about escaping from this Cottage H. You do remember you're in Cottage H now, right?

I say, Oh, right. Cottage H. H is for hell.

That's right, Scotty. You've got it. Now listen, I've got Paleface here with me, and he tells me he's in with us.

Paleface is here?

Of course he's here. He's standing right next to you. What's the matter with you?

This time I shrug before I talk. I say, Oh right. Hi Paleface. Sorry I didn't see you. It's the pills. They're making it so I can't keep things straight anymore. I need to straighten myself out.

Paleface looks at me like he thinks I'm crazy. But I'm not crazy. I may not be up there at the very pinnacle of that normally distributed curve, but I'm not flung way out on the edges either. Didn't I already tell Redtwo that? Or was it that other person. Why is everything so confusing?

Redtwo is touching my arm. I can feel it, so it must be real. He says, listen to Paleface. He's got a plan.

I turn my head, and sure enough, there's Paleface. So he's out here on the screened-in porch too. I say, Hi, Paleface. Do you want to walk with the Cusser and me?

He says, No time for walking now, Scotty. I have something important to tell you. I'm in the CIA.

You are?

Yes, I am. I was placed here to get the goods on Trump, but now it's time for you to get out of here and report back to head-quarters.

I ask, Headquarters? Like the headquarters of the robots?

Paleface shakes his head. He looks like he's exasperated with me. No, he says, I mean CIA headquarters. They need to know what's going on here. Don't you want to get out of this place?

I say, Sure I do. This is Cottage H, and H is for hell.

He nods again. Like Redtwo's shrugs, maybe nodding is what Paleface does when he's about to say something. He says, Right, H is for hell. And I know how to get us out of this hell.

Out of here? I'd like that. In fact, I'd like that a lot. I say, I'm ready. Shall we go now?

He says, Not quite yet. First, we have to put my plan in place. It starts with getting the Growler out of the way. That's your job.

I say, My job?

He nods, which means he's about to talk again. He says, You know, your plan. Your plan to escape.

My plan? Oh right, I'm the one with the plan. He means I'm supposed to think about how to get the Growler out of the way. But how am I supposed to do that?

He's your friend, says Paleface. Use that.

Oh, that's right, I say. My plan was to make him my friend. I've done that, haven't I? Sure I have. Just think.

Okay, I'm supposed to think. But how can I do that with those damn pills messing up my brain? Wait a minute. Pills. That's it. I can use Redtwo's pills. And the milk. I can use the pills and the milk to get the Growler out of the way. It's all coming back to me.

I turn to Redtwo and say, Give me some of your pills.

My pills?

"Yes, the pills in your pocket. How many will I need to knock the Growler out?

Redtwo nods, just like Paleface does when he's about to talk. He says, Oh, right, I get it. But how are you going to get the Growler to take them?

I say, You just leave that to me, Redtwo.

He shrugs, but this time he doesn't talk. Instead, he reaches into his pocket and pulls out a handful of pills. This should do it, he says.

I take the pills and go out to the dayroom to find the Growler.

Of course, he's where he always is, standing against the wall, watching everybody.

I sidle up to him, real casual like, and say, Hi there, my friend Teddy. You know, I'm thirsty, and that rusty water in the restroom is icky. How about we go to the kitchen and have some milk?

He stares at me and whispers, You know about my milk?

Sure I do. A friend knows these things. But Dad Trump doesn't need to know. It'll just be our secret. Aren't you thirsty? Wouldn't a glass of nice cold milk be good right now?

He looks off into the distance. I've got him thinking about it. I say, Let's go have some right now.

He hesitates, but then he turns and starts walking toward the dining room. At the back of the room, he stops, and real sneaky like, peeks around the corner toward Trump's desk.

He's not there. I bet he's in his apartment with a girl.

The Growler leads me though the empty dining room and then into the kitchen area. He takes the bottle of milk out of the refrigerator and hands it to me.

I say, Don't you have any glasses? We should drink out of glasses, like refined people.

He says, Refined?

"Yes, Teddy, I think you are a very refined person, if only other people knew it.

He seems confused by my words, but he does open a cabinet and gets out two red plastic glasses.

I say, Why don't you keep an eye out for Dad Trump while I pour us some milk?

He goes to the kitchen door and opens it just wide enough to peek out.

I quickly pour the two glasses full of milk and put some of Redtwo's pills into one of them. But then I wonder if that's enough. The Growler is a pretty big guy. I go ahead and dump all of the pills into the Growler's glass of milk and stir it with my finger.

The Growler comes back, and I hand him the milk with all the pills in it.

I hold up my glass of milk and say, Now we're supposed to say, Cheers and clink our glasses together.

The Growler doesn't seem to understand, so I just hold up my glass and say, Cheers!

He quickly drinks down his entire glass of milk.

Jesus, I think. I hope taking that many pills all at once doesn't kill him. I only want him to get sleepy. I smile at him and quickly drink my glass of milk. I tastes damn good. How long has it been since I had a glass of milk? Maybe I should pour myself another glassful.

No, I can't get distracted with that. The plan must go forward.

The Growler puts the bottle of milk back into the refrigerator, and we head back to the dayroom. Thankfully, there is still no sign of Trump. Both Redtwo and Paleface are sitting in my usual row, looking totally innocent.

I wink at the Growler and whisper, Thanks, Teddy. That was good.

He goes back to his watching position against the wall, and I go to sit between Redtwo and Paleface.

Redtwo whispers, How'd it go?

I give him thumbs up and say, Now all we have to do is wait.

It takes a lot longer than I would have thought with that many pills in him, but eventually the Growler begins to wobble a bit. He shifts back and forth from foot to foot and starts shaking his head. He doesn't seem to want to give in to what he's feeling.

Redtwo whispers, How many did you give him?

I say, All of them. Isn't that what I was supposed to do?

Redtwo shrugs and says, How am I supposed to know? Maybe it'll kill him.

I tell him, I sure hope not.

Paleface says, Who cares? What's the next step in your plan?

Oh, right, my plan. We can't stop now, no matter what happens to the Growler. The plan must go forward. I say, Lets wait a bit to see what the Growler does.

Both Redtwo and Paleface instantly sit back in their chairs and stay perfectly still. Are they watching the TV? Except for the low murmur of the inane game show contestant voices and the cattle-prod response of the canned laughter, there's not a sound in the dayroom. I've never heard it so quiet. That kind of surprises me, but I guess everybody in the room assumes I'm in charge of the story now, so all they have to do is wait. I figure while we are all waiting to see what the Growler is going to do, I might as well finish my robot book.

All that day at work, Scott was worried about what his robot had learned in response to his direct order to learn about human behavior. He had even made the suggestion that Robot One could run the world better than those ridiculous politicians on the televiewer. The problem was, Robot One had revealed that he was in constant contact with all the other household robots in the world and that he had passed on Scott's suggestion to them. Did that mean the robots were thinking about making themselves look exactly like humans and running for political office?

Scott tried to reassure himself that the robots didn't have the capability to remake themselves. They're not robot manufacturers. But what if they all decide they really are smarter than us humans and that they could do a better job of running the world than us? They might take over the manufacturing plant and modify themselves to look exactly like us humans. We wouldn't be able to tell which ones were the robots and which ones were the humans. What if they decided to take over key jobs and government positions?

Scott couldn't concentrate at work. He was getting more and more worried. What had started out as an interesting project to teach his robot to act more like a human, and his suggestion that they were smarter than humans, might be giving them the idea that really could run the world better than us humans do. Scott decided that he'd better leave work right away and hurry home to try to get his robot to unlearn what he had been teaching it about humans.

Even though the travel tube was fast and it didn't slow down as much that day for ads, it seemed to take forever to get home.

When he got to his building, he took the more expensive express elevator up

to his floor and hurried down the hallway
to his apartment.

He looked in every room, but the
robot was not there. And when he
turned on the televiewer, the lead story
on every network was about the sudden
disappearance of household robots all
over the world.

I see that Growler is having trouble keeping his eyes open.
At least it means he's not a robot, but then we all already knew
that, didn't we?

The Growler seems about to fall down, but he catches himself and shakes his head, hard.

I whisper to Redtwo and Paleface, I think the Growler might
fall down.

Paleface says, So what?

I say, Well, I don't want him to get hurt. He's my friend.

Redtwo stares at me. Your friend? Are you kidding?

Well, he trusted me. He gave me some of his milk, and
besides, this is my story, and I don't want anybody to get hurt. I
should get up and go save him before he falls down and hurts
himself.

Paleface grabs my arm and urgently whispers, No! Let him
fall. He hurt you, didn't he? He whipped the hell out of you. Now
it's his turn to feel what it's like to be hurt.

Paleface has a point, but he doesn't realize that this is my
story, and I've made the Growler, Teddy, my friend. I don't want
it to end with him getting hurt.

I get up and go to him and say, Jeez, Teddy. You look really
tired. I think it's about time for bed, isn't it? Why don't I take you
to bed?

When I grab onto the Growler's arm, for some strange reason, it doesn't feel as huge as before.

I pull him toward the dorm, and when he tries to resist, it
feels like I'm actually stronger than he is. How can that be?

I keep on urging him to walk toward the dorm, and eventually he gets into the rhythm of it, almost as if he's sleepwalking.

When we get to the dorm, I'm not sure which bed to put him in. In fact, I don't know if he even has an assigned bed. I've never seen him sleep.

Then, I see the whipping bed, the one bed set apart from all the others, the bed he tied me to when I was being whipped. I lead him to that bed and coax him into lying down. The cloth strips are still there, and I think about tying him to the bed frame, but then I decide against it. Either my plan to put him to sleep with all those pills is going to work, or it isn't. If he woke up and found himself tied to the bed, he'd probably start yelling and that would bring Trump. No, I'll just leave him here to sleep it off. I don't think he's going to die. He seems to be breathing normally.

On the way back to the dayroom, I wonder if any of the other patients noticed me taking the Growler away.

But when I get there, they all seem to be even more engrossed in the stupid TV than usual. It's as if they somehow all know my plan and know their role is to just sit quietly and stare at the TV. That gives me an odd thought I haven't had before: if the meds haven't turned them into zombies, I bet those mind-numbing TV shows would have done it anyhow.

Redtwo and Paleface are still in their chairs; it's as if they too have been hypnotized by the TV show and haven't moved a muscle

I sit down between them and say, Okay, that went fine. He's back in the dorm sound asleep.

Redtwo is the first one to snap out of it and turn to face me. He blinks a few times, and then says, We've been waiting for you. How did it go?

Didn't he hear me? And Paleface also seems to be a bit out of it. I guess without my plan to tell them what to do, they just don't do anything.

I don't want any of the other patients to hear us talking, so I whisper that we should go out to the screened-in porch to talk.

I lead the way, and they dutifully follow me. I guess they know this is my story, so they just do whatever I tell them.

Once we are out on the screened-in porch, I can't quite think of what the next step in my plan is. For several minutes, I watch the Big Black Cusser walk back and forth, pacing and cussing.

Redtwo says, Isn't it time for the next step?

That snaps me out of it. Oh, right, the next step. That must be Trump. How are we going to deal with Trump?

Paleface says, I can take care of that.

Did I say that part about dealing with Trump out loud? I must have. I say, Okay, Paleface, how do we get the keys from Trump?

He says, Keys? Oh, right, his keys to the Cottage H door. Well, I guess we have to get into his apartment. Is that right?

Yes, I say, we get into his apartment and grab his keys. That's the only way we're going to escape Cottage H.

Redtwo says, No way we can get into his apartment. He keeps his apartment door locked at all times.

Paleface says, I can take care of that. I'll just have one of my secret agents unlock his door, and we'll walk right in and grab his keys.

Did I hear him right? Secret agents?

Sure, he says. I have secret agents all over the place. And one of them is an expert at unlocking doors.

Really? I turn to look at all the other patients. Every one of them seems to be completely hypnotized by the TV. Is it possible that one of these zombie-like patients could be a secret agent? I was a secret agent when I was a kid, wasn't I? Uh, I say, tell me, Paleface, which one of them is your secret agent that's good at unlocking doors?

He points at Catfour.

What? I say. Catfour? He can't even move.

Paleface shrugs. It's not that he can't move, he just doesn't like to move. Besides, he doesn't need to move. He does it with his mind.

His mind? The half-dead-looking Catfour can unlock doors with his mind?

I turn to look at Redtwo, but he only shrugs.

Okay, Paleface, I say, tell him to unlock the door to Trump's apartment.

Paleface says, It's already unlocked. Catfour heard you say you wanted it unlocked, so it is.

This I've got to see, says Redtwo. He starts to get up, but I grab his arm and say, But what if it is unlocked? How are we going to handle Trump? He's bigger than we are, and he's got that damn baseball bat.

Paleface says, I've got the solution to that too. The Big Black Cusser is another one of my secret agents. He can handle Trump.

I watch the Cusser pace back and forth a few times, and then I say, You think you can get through to the Cusser? No way. Believe me, I've tried.

Like I said, says Paleface, he's one of my secret agents. I keep him out here on this screened-in porch so he can stay in constant communication with headquarters.

But Paleface, I say, the Cusser hardly seems to know we're here. He just keeps on walking and cussing.

That's not cussing, says Paleface. It's code. We created a special code that sounds like cussing. Another one of our agents picks up his cussing code words with special high-powered listening equipment. That's why he has to stay out here on this screened-in porch.

I look at Redtwo. Is he going for all this? More likely, Paleface is as crazy as all the other patients on this ward.

Redtwo does what he always does, he shrugs.

I can see you don't believe me, says Paleface. It doesn't matter if you believe me or not, it's true. You'll see. Just follow me and everything will work out in the end. He heads for the door, and when none of us follow, he turns back and says, Well? Don't you want to get out of this Cottage H hell?

Now it's my turn to shrug. Even if he's totally crazy, what can Trump do to us except whip us some more? But now the

Growler is sound asleep in the dorm on the whipping bed, so maybe that option isn't available to Trump anymore. If we get caught, I'll just switch back to my original plan to get all the other patients to gang up on Trump, and we'll take over this ward that way.

I fall into line behind Paleface. Redtwo hesitates, but then he too joins us as we head out the door and to the dayroom.

And then the most amazing thing happens, something so strange that it almost feels like I'm making it up—the Big Black Cusser has stopped walking and cussing, and he's actually following us. Is he really a secret agent? Is his job actually to stay out here on the screen-in porch communicating with CIA headquarters using some kind of weird cussing code?

The three of us go through the dayroom, and not one of the other patients turns away from the TV to watch us go by. It's as if their eyes are somehow attached through the air to that TV screen. Either that, or they somehow know what we're about to do, and they know they're not supposed to interfere with us.

We go straight to the door to Trump's apartment, and the others stand back and wait for me to open the door. Me? Why is it always me that has to confront Trump?

Oh, well, like I said. All he can do is whip me some more. I turn the door's handle, and to my amazement, it really is unlocked. I open the door a crack and peek in. There's not much in the room except a large bed and one chest of drawers against the wall. Trump is in the bed, lying naked on his back, sound asleep and snoring. My first thought at seeing him like that is it was pretty unfair of him to be the one to make fun of the size of *my* protuberance.

Next to him, sitting up in the bed, is a young girl, also naked. She quickly pulls a sheet up in front of herself. He eyes are open very wide, and I can tell she's scared. She's a child, probably no older than twelve.

I put my finger to my lips to tell her to be quiet. She nods and slips out of the bed.

Paleface nods to the Big Black Cusser, and he immediately goes to the bed and grabs both of Trump's arms.

Trump is instantly awake. He tries to sit up, but the Cusser won't let him. Instead of starting to yell, which is what I expect him to do, Trump just stares up at us. He seems to be really scared, actually shaking.

Paleface is already looking for Trump's keys. He finds them in the pants that are hanging from a hook on the wall. He shakes the ring of keys at me, grinning.

Okay, I'm thinking, now we can escape this damn Cottage H. But what to do with Trump?

Paleface again seems to read my thoughts; he says, We could kill him. That'd make sure he doesn't come after you.

No, I say, I don't want the story to end that way.

Paleface says, If we don't kill him, he could call for help.

I notice the phone on the little table next to Trump's bed. It's hooked to the wall by a long cord. I tell Paleface to pull that phone cord out of the wall and use it to tie Trump to his bed.

He does yank the phone cord out of the wall, but then he hands it to the Cusser, who goes right to work tying Trump to the bed.

We hurry out of Trump's room and go right to the door that leads out of Cottage H. I think through the situation. Assuming the Growler is still asleep in the dorm, we can use Trump's keys to walk right out of here. Wait a minute, I say, what if someone sees us leaving here? Won't they just grab us and bring us right back?

Paleface says, No problem, just walk down the hill as if you do it every day. There's a little town down there, and patients from the open wards go down there to get ice cream and stuff like that. Just act natural, like you do it all the time.

But won't the guards notice a group like us, hurrying down the hill all together?

Oh, no, says Paleface, me and the Cusser have to stay here. Our CIA assignment is this ward. You have to go alone.

Alone? I say. But why did you work so hard getting the keys?

He just shrugs.

I turn to Redtwo and say to him, What about you? You said you wanted to get out of here before you turned into a zombie like all the others. Don't you want to go with me?

Naw, he says with a shrug. Out there, I might get violent again. This is your plan, so you should go alone. We'll be fine here now that we've got control of Trump and the Growler. I'll take care of Trump personally.

What do you mean, take care of him?

Paleface steps between us. Not your worry, he says. Just go. He unlocks the door and pushes the naked girl out. She runs away, fast.

Then, he tries to push me out, but I say, Where am I supposed to go? Back to the library? Back to that bar?

No, he says, it's time for you to go home. Just head down the hill, and Barefoot Billy will be waiting there to take you home.

Barefoot Billy?

Paleface nods. Didn't I tell you? He's another one of my agents.

But wait, I say, I'm not so sure I'm ready to just walk out of here without thinking it through. I've been here so long, it seems like . . . uh, where I belong.

It's not where you belong, says Paleface, and he continues to try to push me out.

No, I say. I'm not leaving until I find out what you're going to do with Trump. And what about all the other patients? Don't they want to escape too?

Redtwo shakes his head and says, Naw, they wouldn't know what to do without their TV and their breakfast cereal and their afternoon sandwiches. You just go along. He turns to the Cusser and gives him some kind of hand signal.

Without a word, the Big Black Cusser pushes me out onto the sidewalk.

Paleface pulls the door closed, and I hear the door lock.
I bang on the door with both of my fists.

"Now wait a minute, this is not my plan. I'm not ready to leave."

"I'm afraid you have no choice, Mr. Scott. Your observation period is over, and we need your bed for other patients. Your father will be waiting for you outside this door. He will take you home."

"Home? Do I still have a home besides Cottage H?"

"Of course you do, Mr. Scott. You and I both know your so-called Cottage H doesn't really exist. And your father is eager to get you back home where he can take care of you."

"But."

"Now, now, Mr. Scott, there is nothing to worry about once you are outside outside of this door. As soon as we let you go, you'll see there is a real world outside, and there is a place for you in it. We gave your father a prescription for you. It's pills. If you take them as directed, you'll soon forget there ever was a place you thought of as Cottage H."

"But . . . but, what about the Growler? He's my friend now. And will the Big Black Cusser ever get to go find his wife in Chicago?"

"They will all be fine without you, Mr. Scott. Your task now is to take your new meds every day and let your father take care of you."

"Oh, sure, that's what they said the last time. What if he turns me over to the robots? What if he is a robot?"

"Oh, right, your robot book. You can still do that. Your father says he bought you a brand new writing notebook. It's in your room at home. You can stay there and write your book about the robots. I'm afraid we can't let you ever publish it, but you can write about it all you want. Now that you've been officially diagnosed as a paranoid schizophrenic, nobody will take the idea seriously that we are actually taking over."

"Ah hah! I knew you were a robot from the first moment I laid eyes on you. Too smooth, and your office was too much like what I expected it to be."

"Now, now, Mr. Scott. No more of that. You don't want to end up back in Cottage H, do you? Best thing for you now is to just go home with your father and write your little book. Take your meds, and keep your focus on reality, and everything will be fine. Goodbye now. I hope to never to see you back in here again. Do you understand?"

She's still using her smooth shrink voice, but I can tell she's threatening me. She thinks she can threaten me with Trump and all of her other robot cohorts, and that will keep me under control. But what she doesn't know, is that I actually am going to write my book, and I'm going to write it so much like an interesting story that everybody will want to read it.

I'll tell the truth about her and Barefoot Billy and Trump and the Growler and the Big Black Cusser and Redtwo and Paleface and all the others. And everybody *will* believe me. I'm sure of it.

www.ingramcontent.com/pod-product-compliance
Lightning Source LLC
Chambersburg PA
CBHW071235130626
46556CB00003B/1021